THE GOVERNESS

DANA MITCHELL

The Governess

By Dana Mitchell
Copyright © 2020 Dana Mitchell

Cover design and formatting by Exposed Publishing

DEDICATION

*To Josie Baker, Ree Thornton, Sara Hartland, LJ Langdon
and Elsa Holland:
A fine group of ladies who are superlative writers, and
even more superlative as friends.*

*To Rachel Bailey, for sharing her wonderful, extensive and
fabulous knowledge to help shape this book. And her salt
and vinegar chips.*

*To the incomparable Morgana McLeod, for all your help,
patience, encouragement and cheese over many, many
years.
Bless you all.*

CHAPTER ONE

Scottish Highlands – End of Winter 1748

Frances Rothbury swallowed as she viewed the sullen sky. The approaching storm clouds heralded bad weather. Her gaze went to the fast disappearing crofter who'd left her in the middle of the empty road after some garbled speech and hand waving in the direction of the river. It seemed just a moment ago, she'd been enjoying the sunshine and fresh air. Now, in the sudden darkening of the day, the breath she drew in was as unsteady as her future.

She had to find Laird Grant and Muckrach castle, and quickly.

A muted splash broke the silence and she spun around, her thumb rubbing the handle of her bag as her gaze searched the woodland at the edge of the road. The crofter had pointed in the direction of the river. *The Laird would be fishing.* The thought popped into her mind and used to heeding her intuition, she nodded. The River Dulnain was known for its salmon.

Walking off the road and down the overgrown, narrow track, she approached the bank of the river, trying to picture what the Laird would look like. Sighing, she let herself hope that he was kind. Perhaps he'd be thin and wiry, with grey hair and burly sideburns, and a twinkle in his eye.

This close, the water of the river swirled in big lazy circles. Its current deep and fast in the middle, the water dark and metallic, reflecting the clouds. Distant thunder rumbled, adding to the waiting quality of the air.

There was no one, either in the water, or out.

Aware of the deep silence, Frances inhaled silently as the hairs on her neck stood up. She took a careful, quiet step back.

He didn't come up in a rush, needing to inhale like a mere mortal.

He came up as though part of the water, like a river God, choosing then to separate himself to the atmosphere. Water sheeted off his dark hair, licking down the masculine planes of his face. The more he surged forward, the more his glistening, muscular frame emerged. He strode toward the bank, his light-coloured eyes focused solely on her.

Her fingers tightened around the handle of her bag. It should have been painful because of the blisters on her palms inside her ruined gloves. No pain registered as she gazed with unblinking fascination at the entity rising out of the river.

A *naked* entity.

A chaste woman would have at least turned her head in a display of modesty. The only other naked man she'd seen had not been built like this. Her riveted gaze marked the comparison between the fleshy, pudgy Lord who'd tried to rape her only weeks ago, and this formidable specimen of manhood. The muscles of his abdomen were clearly defined in the eerie light.

Her wide-eyed gaze travelled lower and then skittered across to where a salmon barely thrashed in his big hand as he stopped at the bank.

Frances blinked and looked up.

He radiated intelligent curiosity as he returned her gaze, not bothering to hide his nudity. For a moment, they stared at one another, the silence like a cocoon. She took a step back, and then another, heartened by the fact he didn't move.

But then the intensity of his focus increased, and he stepped forward.

And in that instant, it all changed.

The cold came first, a frost that concentrated in her heart and then burned with each beat in her blood. "No," she whispered in despair, but the fire spread through her bloodstream like an icy blaze.

She took five rapid backward steps, gasping for breath.

Tossing the salmon, the man started for her.

Frances whirled and ran.

The metallic taste in her mouth made her run harder. Trying to control the *beserker* that increased her strength and numbed her mind was impossible. Oh, God. It was happening again. *And she couldn't stop it.*

"Stop!"

There was command in that deep Scottish brogue, but Frances kept running. It was the only way she could save him. He didn't deserve to die. He hadn't looked remotely lecherous. The only crime he'd committed was nudity, but in his form, that was no crime.

"I'll not hurt you, lass!"

Frances heard his shouted words but still ran, risking a terrified peek over her shoulder—

His large hand almost at her shoulder frightened whatever wits that hadn't already vacated their precarious position. She surged forward.

And then those hard fingers grasped her shoulder

and Frances screamed. Her arm swung as she lashed out.

"Ow!"

They went down in a tangle of arms and legs. Somehow, she landed on top, her damp gloves skidding over smooth, wet, naked skin as she tried to get purchase against the bulging muscles of his chest. When that didn't work, she arched her back, using the strength of her entire body to dislodge the strong arm wrapped around her waist.

It didn't budge; he wasn't even breathing hard, the whole episode completed in silence. That scared Frances more than if he'd grunted like an animal.

She whimpered, wondering why the *beserker* hadn't yet taken over.

With a whirl, she was tumbled over, her back hitting the soft grass with enough force to make her gasp. Gritting her teeth, she clenched her fists against his shoulders to keep him at bay and scrunched her eyes shut. *She couldn't bear to see another person die...*

"I'll not hurt you, lass. Can you understand?"

She heard the words over the rapid tattoo of her heart and the breath rushing in and out of her lungs. She would lose herself, unconscious to the *beserker* taking over her body, her reason, it's strength and purpose entirely devoted to defending herself to the death.

"There now, calm yourself. You be safe."

Safe? Despite his body crushing hers into the grass, it wasn't herself she was worried about. He was oblivious to the mortal danger. The ancient, cursed affliction she bore would roar into life and vanquish him, just as it had with the rapacious Lord.

Yet...

Nothing happened.

Even as she expected it to build, the metallic taste in her mouth and the cold seeping into her muscles started to wane. Frances lay, agog beneath his solid weight, trying to breathe.

Her faculties were intact. For the first time ever, the *beserker* withdrew. Tears spurted behind her closed eyes; the relief was so enormous she took in a sobbing breath. All she could do was lay there, beneath a very large, very naked man.

Awareness skyrocketed as she felt every single inch of his hard body against hers. Felt, too, the strength in his muscles as her hands still curled into his shoulders to keep him at bay. Muscles that were barely using a fraction of their true strength.

She shivered in the aftermath, at his mercy.

"Lass, are you alright?" His voice softened. "I'm sorry if I hurt you."

Giving a jerky nod, she didn't know what else to do.

A soft caress against her cheekbone had her drawing in a startled breath and she opened her eyes. Frances could only stare at him as his deep voice seemed to vibrate into her very bones. Her arms gradually relaxed as his thumb swept over the skin of her cheekbone as though he loved its fine, silky texture.

"It's best never to run from a naked man. Not when his reputation is at stake."

Humour crinkled the skin next to his light grey eyes, one side of his lips canting in a wry half-smile. He pushed himself up off her, grasping her hand to pull her up.

She tried to firm the wobble in her knees and risked a peek, thankful he'd grasped an article of his clothing to shield his masculinity.

"You caught me unawares. And without a stitch on, to boot. If I hadn't tripped like a clumsy clod, we would no' have hit the ground."

The soft brogue delivered in his deep voice with a

hint of humour was pleasing, a bass rumble. Some of her clenched muscles released their tension and her lungs loosened to take a better breath.

"You're sure you're alright?"

She nodded, her gaze drawn to the blood on his mouth.

Her aimless clout as he'd grabbed her had been spot-on. Blood welled, snaking in a thin trail to pool into a ruby droplet at the edge of his bottom lip. Unable to take her eyes off it, she watched as the questing probe of his tongue investigated the wound.

His gaze was on her, and in an instant, awareness struck in a primitive rush as the curiosity morphed into a wry, masculine survey. "There's nothing wrong with your aim. Who are you, lass? What are you doing here, on my land?"

Finally, she remembered to look away and spoke in breathless tones to the nearby tree. "Begging your pardon, Sir. I'm sorry for trespassing, and for striking you."

"You're English." His tone changed; the humour and warmth disappeared.

"Yes. I-I'm the new governess, here to see Laird Grant." She heard a rustle of cloth.

"I dinna ask for a governess."

The voice was closer, and her gaze wrenched back to his. *He was the Laird?* The kind, wiry gentleman she'd envisioned faded. The man had donned on a kilt, covering his loins. Frances was grateful, but her gaze was drawn to the muscles of his chest and arms. That he was barefoot did not detract from his overwhelming masculinity. He had no spare fat anywhere. Her gaze skittered back to his face to find it unsmiling, his eyes narrowed.

And it seemed, no spare kindness.

She raised her chin, covering her panic at his words with a tremulous smile. Giving a small curtsy, she introduced herself. "My name is Frances Sp… Rothbury. Pleased to meet you."

Frances could have kicked herself. Covering her tracks had meant changing her surname from Spencer to Rothbury. Still unused to it, she'd nearly slipped up.

He frowned, then narrowed his gaze as he reiterated, "I dinna ask for a governess. Best you be heading home."

Home. Her teeth clenched together. *She had no home.* "But my agency has supplied as requested."

"I haven't—," he said, then hissed out a breath. "You said you were here to see the Laird? Laird who?"

The implacable tone was backed up by a rumble of thunder. The storm had crept closer.

Frances straightened. "Laird Grant. Laird Angus Grant."

A muscle jumped in his jaw as he nodded. "Aye, my father. He died two months ago."

With that, he turned and walked back to the rest of his clothes, shrugged on his shirt and pulled on his boots. Scooping up the salmon and his sword tied with leather, he then stalked toward the road—as though she didn't exist.

Scrambling for her bag, Frances trotted after him, addressing his back. "I'm very sorry for your loss…?"

"Duncan. Duncan Grant. I'm the Laird, now."

"Beg pardon, Laird. But I've come all this way, for a legitimate request of employment," she protested, juggling her bag as she tried to keep up with his large stride.

"Go back to where you've come from. You're not welcome here."

Thunder rumbled in the distance, a menacing back up to a statement that brooked no argument. To hear it said nearly broke her spirit.

Nearly.

They reached the road and Frances tried again, using her most placatory tone. "Laird Grant, please, I'm sure we can work this out. Surely your wife—"

"My wife is dead."

He strode on. Gritting her teeth, she puffed as she increased her trot. "I'm sorry to hear Laird. Please, even if I wanted to, I have no means of travel to the nearest town, no money for lodgings—"

He stopped so suddenly she nearly ran into him. Wide-eyed, she backed up.

His gaze narrowed. "Why here? Why would an English woman, a *Sassenach*, come to the wilds?" He gestured to the storm, "To this heathen place, to be a governess?"

Swallowing, Frances lowered her lashes, unable to face the suspicion in his grey eyes.

He must never know.

Lifting her gaze, she raised her chin. "I do not believe you are heathen, Laird Grant. And my assumption would be correct since you have need of a governess."

He arched a brow. "Not many English men venture into these parts, Miss Rothbury, unless they're wearing a red coat. I'm sure you'd be aware, too, as an English woman in the highlands, you're a very rare commodity."

She frowned. "What do you mean? I'm a governess, and nothing more."

His gaze bored into hers. "I'm not even sure *how* you managed to get here, travelling alone. Tell me, did no one question you?"

"No." She told the truth, no one had questioned her Englishness, because she'd faked a Scottish accent if spoken to, which was twice. Faked her name also, although she'd nearly given it away when she'd introduced herself. Desperate times called for desperate measures.

Distrust gleamed in his grey eyes. "I don't believe you. I think you're a spy."

A spy?

Frances blinked. "A spy?" She shook her head. "I can assure you Laird Grant; I am no such thing. I have a letter from the Agency confirming my employment. And I can show you when we get to the castle. The storm is fast approaching."

He appeared not to care about the storm, never taking his eyes off hers. The waning light had cast shadows near his cheekbones and eyes. His broad shoulders seemed to loom; it was almost as though he surrounded her.

The ice around her heart pulsed as his expression remained unchanged. She couldn't help stuttering, "P-please, Laird, surely in this weather even a stray dog would find shelter at your castle?"

For the longest moment, he stood resolute and unmoving. And then he said softly, "Aye. A stray dog."

Her lips tightened at the insult, but she raised her chin higher and held his gaze.

The Laird turned away, speaking over his shoulder, "Come Miss *Rothbury*, if its shelter you seek, then shelter can be provided. For a short time."

Thunder cut short her sigh of relief; it's rolling rumble echoing her misgivings despite securing shelter from the coming storm. She let out a breath as she again followed his long stride, seeing the turrets of Muckrach castle for the first time in the distance.

Her gaze couldn't help focusing on his broad shoulders and her mouth pursed as she tried to keep up, buoyed by a sudden thought:

At least she hadn't killed him.

CHAPTER TWO

Woken early the next morning by two scamps who'd come to investigate the *sassenach*, Frances blinked to clear the sleep from her eyes, eager to prove her natural ability with children. The Laird had been polite but distant the previous night and she was desperate to prove her worth.

Her bedroom was luxury compared to what she was used to. A rug on the floor and fire blazing in the hearth. The bed smelled fresh with thick covers to ward off the chill. Frances had never been so grateful for a bed in her life, and for once, had slept dreamlessly.

Rummaging beneath the covers, she quickly untied the knot of the rope around her wrist that bound her to the bed, and, as the children entered, left it hidden beneath the sheets.

Roslyn was eight. She was so beautiful, Frances experienced an ache in her heart she'd never felt before. Frances helped her up on the bed and just like that, they became firm friends.

Brodie was ten, with his father's light grey eyes. He held back, his expression impassive. "How did you get here?" he demanded, "My father doesn't like *sassenachs*. I don't either."

"I came by a coach, a crofter's cart and by foot. And I'm just a person, Master Brodie."

"That's rude, Brodie," Roslyn admonished and then touched the ends of Frances' hair. "Will my hair ever grow as long as yours? It's so pretty."

"Of course it will, little sparrow. You'll be so beautiful your father will make all your suitors line up around Muckrach Castle in the hope of winning your fair hand."

Roslyn wrinkled her nose and shook her head. "Not boys."

"What's wrong with boys?" demanded Brodie. Sidling closer, he leaned against the edge of the bed.

"They smell and have dirt on the face *all the time.*"

Brodie rolled his eyes and shook his head with exasperation.

Frances chuckled. He was a confusing mix with his father's eyes, but the exact reaction that her brother would have shown. Her beloved brother who'd protected her right up until he'd died from scarlet fever.

She smothered a sad smile.

If he were still here, she wouldn't be in so much trouble...

Blinking quickly to banish her ghosts, she smiled brightly down at the angel nestled in her arms.

"Our Grandpapa died."

Frances made a sympathetic sound and hugged Roslyn. "I'm very sorry to hear that sad news."

Roslyn nodded. "He used to make me laugh all the time and let me sit on his knee. Do you have a Grandpa?"

Frances shook her head. "No, I don't have a Grandpa."

"I don't have a Mama, either. She died too, when I was little. Do you have a Mama, Miss Wotherbury?"

Frances hesitated, then shook her head. "No darling, I have no family."

Frowning, Roslyn curled her little hand around Frances'. "But that means you have no one. You can join our family, can't she Brodie? It must be lonely."

Smiling, Frances didn't answer. Brodie watched her, his face grave.

Roslyn stroked the tips of Frances' long hair with shining eyes. "Miss Wotherbury—"

"Rothbury, little sparrow, with an 'r'."

"Come, children. You know better than to disturb guests."

Frances started at the deep voice from the open doorway. The early morning shadows hugged the laird's face, giving it a forbidding countenance.

"But, Papa, I can't say the 'r'," Roslyn complained.

"You will with lots of practice," soothed Frances.

"I hope you stay, Miss Wotherbury."

"I would love to stay." Frances couldn't help the small defiance.

"It's time to pack your things, Miss Rothbury. Come Roslyn."

Even as her heart sank, Frances gave the child a slight nudge, but she refused to move

"Now, Roslyn."

Roslyn scrambled off the bed at his stern voice and Frances immediately missed her warmth. Both children looked at her before darting around their father, who filled the doorway. She could hear Roslyn's plaintive voice clearly from the hallway.

"It's not fair! I like her. Her eyes talk and she smiles. She wasn't like the last one—"

"Be quiet, Roslyn," Brodie grumbled in a long-suffering tone.

"But Papa promised we would have a gov'ness."

Their voices grew fainter as they filed up the hallway and then turned the corner.

So. He had need of a governess after all.

Filled with a little more hope, Frances wriggled to the side of the big bed, trying to keep her feet well beneath her robe. The promise of a mild winter was a promise not kept. It had continued to rain overnight, heavy, interspersed with thunder and lightning, and the cold had crept in swiftly.

"Laird Grant, tha—"

"Like you said last night, you sought shelter, just as any mongrel stray would during a storm."

"Thank you." Proud of her firm voice, she pretended not to hear the slur, pretended she was dressed and that she wasn't still in her robe, the ends of her hair curling halfway down her back, her face still warm from her pillow.

He dismissed her thanks with an arched brow, looking over her head to the curtains pulled back to let in the meagre light. "You leave today, after breakfast."

The door shut with a decisive click behind him as he left and her shoulders slumped. She couldn't go back to London. Even now, Lord Ashburn's men would be looking for her; who knew if they'd found her trail? Oh, how she wanted to doubt they would have followed her to Scotland, but she did not have the luxury of that confidence.

Not when she'd killed a Lord.

Her lips trembled as she allowed herself a moment to wallow, smoothing her thumb over her barely healed, blistered palms.

If only—

She straightened and inhaled deeply before letting it out. Her hand slid beneath the covers for the small length of rope and untied the other end, shaping it into a small coil. It was the only way to prevent her sleep walking, a lifeline to hide her affliction. *More like afflictions. Plural.*

Frances sighed and proceeded to dress and pack. The trembling lips, however, took much longer to master. But, by the time she presented herself to the kitchen, a determined, sunny smile cheered her face. It stayed there as she ate her porridge.

The kitchen teemed with movement and warmth; rosy-faced children and the yeasty smell of bread being made and baked in the large ovens. Beyond, she could see the rain pouring down in a drab, grey veil and wondered how the Laird could turn her out in such weather.

As though she conjured him from her thoughts, he appeared at the doorway, this time flanked by other men. One, as tall as the Laird, and just as broad but dark-haired caught her attention. Even if his expression didn't convey his dislike, she would have been dumb not to realise it. Drawing in a deep breath, she straightened her spine, prepared for what was coming. But despite that, it was still a jolt when the Laird's gaze captured hers.

The expression on his face reminded her of when he'd risen from the river; unsmiling and intent. Only now she wasn't frightened out her wits and he wasn't naked, and she realised the jolt was attraction. Uncomfortable, she focused instead on the way they wore a leather belt strapped over one shoulder, another one low down around the waist.

As he made his way over, his men followed. In full dress with kilts, coats and boots, and swords in their scabbards, they were a formidable sight.

On his approach, she rose and curtsied. "Laird Grant."

"Miss Rothbury."

Firming her lips, she waited.

"You're packed, then?"

She nodded once. "Yes."

He nodded, too, looking through the door to the

grey veil over the land outside the castle, and those who scurried in from the damp cold, warming their hands near the fire. Letting out a breath, he gave her a narrowed look. "I'll not be turning you out in such weather. You'll stay until the rain stops. We'll provide your food and shelter until then."

Frances curtsied again, relief expanding like golden light inside her. "I am grateful beyond measure, Laird Grant, thank you for kindness. I'll see to the children immediately."

Hope soared, the tightness in her chest easing slightly as he nodded and continued on his way. Allowing a small smile, she called out the children and proceeded as she knew best.

~

The rain ceased before lunch two days later. Before the drops in the sky had stopped falling, she'd seen the Laird in the large hall. With him the dark-haired man who so disliked her.

Malcolm.

He gestured to her and they both looked over at her. Discomforted, Frances dropped her gaze to her hands, folded in her lap. The muscles in her stomach tensed. The darkness emanating from Malcolm had nothing to do with the colour of his hair.

She didn't have to wait long.

"Miss Rothbury, you're packed?"

She looked up at the Laird's voice, her careful expression impassive. "Yes, Laird."

He nodded, and a muscle jumped in his jaw. "Good. Gill, the crofter who gave you a lift the other day will be by later. He'll take you on to Granttown."

Disappointment rose. Still, she couldn't help but be grateful for the transport. "You have been very kind, Laird Grant."

He glanced down at her hands, then his narrowed gaze sought hers. "I thought not having to carry your bag might give a bit more time for your blisters to heal."

Startled by his quiet observation, she carefully curled her fingers around her palms and then nodded again. "Yes. Thank you."

He left with his men, a sudden break in the clouds making the last of the rain falling glitter like drops of fire. She watched him until he disappeared.

The housekeeper put a plate in front of her and bade her to eat. "Gill is eating too, so dinna worry about leaving just yet. We've been able to get a good portion of the week's tasks done, Miss Rothbury, thanks to you keeping the children occupied."

Frances smiled, "My pleasure Mrs Cullen."

Mrs Cullen looked away for a moment and then called out, "Master Brodie! Away from the ovens if you please. I keep tellin' you it's not a place for playing!"

Giving an exasperated sigh, the housekeeper hurried toward the Laird's son. Frances tucked into her meal, grateful for the food. She didn't know when she'd be eating next and any food was welcome.

She looked up the large hall. Lots of people were eating; clearly this was a working estate.

All too soon she was leaving with the crofter in his cart. Roslyn clung to her hand, in tears this time and Mrs Cullen lifted the little girl away, hugging her close to her side. She gave Frances a small cloth bundle and whispered, "Some cheese and bread for your journey, Miss Rothbury."

Frances looked into the weathered face of the other woman, her eyes filling with tears of gratitude at the kindness. "Thank you, Mrs Cullen," she whispered as squeezed the other woman's fingers hard.

It didn't take too long to get to Granttown, Gill

the crofter setting a much faster pace than the previous day. The cobblestones were slippery with the recent rain, but the clouds had cleared. The little town was tidy, and most people seemed respectable. Some of her anxiety and fear lifted when she spied the church.

Without thinking, she immediately changed course and nearly ran into a band of red coats. Her countrymen, although two of them viewed her with less-than savoury glances, leering as they cantered past, slowing down at the back of the pack.

She watched them with a wary gaze, the wariness increasing when they slowed enough to ride next to her.

"Ma'am." One of them doffed his tricorn.

Frances gave a short nod and kept walking.

"Oh, ho! Too good for the likes of us she is, Rob."

"Can't even give us so much as a by your leave."

The one called Rob was the one to watch. His insolent gaze travelled from her face, down to her bodice. His nose had at least once been broken during a previous fight and a scar divided his right eyebrow. Even compared to his companion, he was unkempt, a dirty kerchief about his neck.

But it was meanness in his bloodshot eyes that was the worst. Frances walked faster even though she knew she couldn't escape them, her fingers tightening around the handle of her bag until they ached.

"You're alone, aren't ya love? We can be friendly-like."

The leering one guffawed.

Frances swallowed. "No, thank you. I'm not alone."

Surprise flashed across their faces as one of them exclaimed, "You're English!"

She didn't answer, increasingly hemmed in by the

horses, until they had her against the front of a garden hedge.

"Please move, you're blocking my path." She wanted to sound sharp and annoyed, instead she sounded scared and breathless.

They chuckled. Rob leaned down and touched grimy fingers to the skin of her neck.

She knocked his hand away. "Don't touch me!" she hissed.

His body odour hit her nostrils and arched away, trying not to breathe through her nose.

They laughed, but all she could hear was malice.

Frances froze as ice filled her veins. *Oh, God—*

"Hoi! You two! What the *blazes* are you doing?" An officer cantered up; his face thunderous as he gave both men a verbal serve.

The relief was overwhelming. She took a deep breath as her lungs loosened but gave no indication of her sudden dizziness other than a couple of rapid blinks.

"My apologies, Ma'am." The officer tipped his hat and all three of them cantered off.

Frances inhaled an unsteady breath as watched them leave. Rob looked back, and his expression made her stomach turn. Her senses rioted and her groping fingers found a sturdy branch in the hedge. All her focus turned inwards, despite her best efforts to control it.

She shuddered as images of unknown women, their faces bruised, bloodied, some so obviously dead, flashed in her mind.

Scrunching her eyes up tightly, she muttered, "No, no no."

On occasion throughout her life, this happened but she had learned to control her dismay and tamp it down until the images disappeared. She had too many other concerns to allow anything else to cause more distress.

After a small moment, her mind was blessedly clear. She collected herself and hurried on toward the church. It was late afternoon and imperative that she find lodgings soon, although she didn't know how she was going to pay for them.

The village priest was sympathetic to her plight, his kind eyes full of concern. He could only provide lodgings for the night but had news that a neighbouring clan Laird might have need of a governess for their children. It was a long shot, but one she was desperate to try.

To repay his kindness, she set about helping the priest with whatever he needed, fetching water from the well and other menial tasks as he bade. She would do anything not to be out in the darkness, alone.

~

*D*uncan cantered into Granttown and pulled to a stop, surveying the main street in the waning light.

"She could be anywhere."

"Aye, Laird, where do you suppose she's staying the night? Maybe at the inn?"

The speaker's tone was hopeful, followed by a chorus of ayes, no doubt for a pint. The light had nearly gone but he wasn't worried. He knew she wouldn't have gone far. No money, no employment. She'd still be here.

"Remind me again, Laird, why you've hauled our arses into town at this fine hour of the day to find a lowly *Sassenach* wench?"

There were a few guffaws, but most remained silent. Malcolm had been with him since they were wee lads, had grown with him. There were inseparable until Duncan's father had sent Duncan to boarding school in England. But that hadn't changed the depth of their friendship. Malcolm was like a brother. He spoke in sarcastic tones like a brother, too.

Duncan turned with a half grin. "I can just as sooner make you look after my children, Malcolm. A fine wet nurse you'd make."

All the men laughed, especially when Malcolm offered a rare grin as he swore.

Looking around, Duncan thought for a moment and then nudged his horse for the church. As he walked his horse and listened to the idle conversation of his men, he wondered about Miss Rothbury. Wondered about her story.

What type of governess spoke of murder and Lords in their sleep, and tied themselves to their bed?

In the hour before dawn, he'd checked to ensure she was still abed, suspicious of her presence, and her story. He'd bet she was hiding something. On approaching her door, he'd heard her cry out, so he'd knocked on the door and called out her name. But she'd not responded further. It was only for her own safety that he'd opened the door, unsure as to whether she was suffering some sort of ague.

In the meagre light of the candle, he'd watched her, in the throes of a nightmare. Her pretty features contorted and her hands coming up as though holding an object in both hands. He'd seen the thin rope tied around her wrist, but he'd been more captivated by that stubborn chin, her sharp cheekbones and her fierce expression.

If she'd been awake, he'd wonder if her eyes would burn blue as they had down at the river. For a moment he wondered if he were seeing things as she'd whirled to run. And then instinct took over. By the time he'd caught her, her eyes had been screwed shut, but when she opened them, they were the most perfect, dazzling blue.

Coupled with her dark hair, she was a striking woman. 'Aye, a striking, bloody English woman," he muttered to himself. He let out an audible breath as they stopped at the church and dismounted. He banged on the door, and after a while heard someone bustling.

The door opened and the father's face appeared. "Laird Grant! What a surprise."

"Father, sorry to interrupt your peace. I've come to talk with Miss Rothbury, if she's here."

"Ah. Well, of course," the priest said, "Come in, come in. We were just sitting down to the evening meal. There's plenty to share."

Duncan walked in and shut the door. "Actually, I won't stay. And neither will Miss Rothbury. The light is nearly gone."

"Oh?"

They walked into the kitchen and Frances immediately stood and curtsied. "Laird Grant."

"Miss Rothbury, apologies for the interruption." He couldn't help but stare. If anything, she'd grown prettier than he remembered.

"Not at all, how can I help?"

He took a deep breath. "It seems I may have to renege on my decision not to hire you."

"Oh?" she replied, her face a blank mask.

He could read nothing from her expression. "Aye. It seems in the short time you visited castle Muckrach, you did everything to ensure the day would go correctly and now none can do without your guidance."

"I doubt it, Laird. I would say it's just the novelty of a new face."

Duncan inclined his head. "No, apparently not. Roslyn is inconsolable, and Mrs Cullen has been muttering dire warnings, more so than normal."

The priest harrumphed and coughed, but his eyes twinkled, and Duncan winked. "Aye, Father, if that were possible."

He turned his gaze back to the woman standing so still, no smile softening her face. Her eyes were like the clearest, deepest sapphire against the foil of her dark hair.

She was beautiful.

He cleared his throat. "Miss Rothbury, I must ask you to consider coming back to the castle, as governess for my children.

For a moment, everyone was silent, with only the hiss and pop of the wood burning in the hearth.

And as it extended, his gaze narrowed into her. "Miss Rothbury?" he prompted, a hint of steel in his tone.

She raised her chin. "I'll consider your offer, upon the condition that the late Laird Grant's original terms be amended.

Duncan raised a brow. "Oh?"

The priest cleared his throat uncomfortably.

"Yes. I wish to have two allotted days off per month."

Duncan took a step toward her, incredulous that she would even think to negotiate with him. "Two full days?"

The chin went higher, and he could see the workings of her throat beneath her fine, pale skin as she swallowed.

"Yes. And no change to my stipend."

The lass was as brazen as you like. He could walk out now and leave her with nothing but the clothes on her back, yet she stood there, calmly negotiating her contract.

"And why would you think I'd agree?"

"Because as you say, Roslyn is inconsolable. And

none can make the day go correctly or do without my guidance."

Duncan looked at the priest, who raised his brows and manfully tried not to smile.

Grinding his teeth, he nodded, reluctance dripping off every one of his words. "Aye. Alright, I agree."

She turned to the priest. "Father, you witnessed the Laird's agreement."

Duncan inhaled and skewered her with a sharp look. "Careful, lass. I don't go back on my word once given. You'd best be remembering that."

Swallowing, she nodded. "Thank you, Laird Grant. Yes, I will take up your offer."

A kind of dark satisfaction filled him at her words, something he did not want to acknowledge. But it was too strong to ignore. Since he'd first laid eyes on her at the river, she was like an itch just beneath his skin. When she'd left, something hadn't felt right, a feeling deep within that wouldn't be denied. She would be in his castle now, where he could keep an eye on her properly.

In a gruff voice, he said, "We need to leave now, t'will be dark before we get back to the castle."

Surprise flashed across her expression. "We're leaving *now*. Riding i-in the dark?"

He watched her closely. "Aye. It won't take long; we'll be on horseback with the men. Sterrm could get us home with his eyes shut."

"Sterrm?"

He gave her a small smile. "Aye, my horse. It means 'stars.'"

She nodded. "What a lovely name for a horse."

Duncan saw her draw in a deep breath. Then she returned his gaze. "I'll go get my things."

So. She didn't like the dark. He filed the information away for later consideration.

Soon they were outside, where his men waited. They boosted her on Sterrm and she clutched at her skirts to ensure her modesty. Duncan settled in behind her, his mouth quirking with no humour when every muscle in her body went rigid.

In the space of twenty-four hours it was the second time their bodies had touched. And now, his awareness of her as a woman was hard to ignore; the softness of her bottom nestled against him, her sweet scent.

Since his wife's death in childbirth with Roslyn, he'd not been celibate, but he'd chosen carefully. His English wife had been fragile, and despite her never complaining, the rough, cold climate had not been good for her constitution. He'd not loved Marie, but he'd cared for her as best he could.

Aye, English women weren't meant for the likes of him, and not for the hard, Scottish conditions. Besides, he'd done what his father had wanted, and married an English. Now his wife, and his father were dead, and he was free to make his own decisions.

They did not include weak English women.

They bid the priest good night and started back though town. Miss Rothbury held herself so stiffly away from him, it was a wonder her backbone didn't crack—

"Halt!"

Duncan steadied his horse with ease as it shied a little before settling in front of the two English red coats. "A fine evening to you, gentlemen. What can I do you for?"

He felt Frances stiffen and she unconsciously moved back against him. Duncan took a closer look at the officers, watching their eyes, their expression. One had a cold, avid gleam in his eyes as he fixed them unceasingly on Frances.

Duncan tightened his hands around the reins as his arms contracted to tuck her closer to him. That she let him told him plenty about the situation, and that dark satisfaction rose again as she sought protection in his arms.

"Where are taking this woman?"

Before he could speak, one of his men piped up.

"Where are ye manners, yer red-coated slugs. It be the Laird Grant yer talking to!"

"Hush Fergus," Duncan bade his man on the right then fixed a level stare at the red-coat. "What's the woman to you, lad?"

Someone spat, the sound loud in the silence and Duncan knew it was Malcolm.

Duncan heard Frances audibly swallow. The air thickened with tension, which only increased as more officers spilled out of the inn, blocking the street.

"We know she's English. What do you want with her? You're holding her against her will."

The silence was so thick, it was choking.

"What say you, Miss Rothbury? Are we holding you against your will?"

～

Frances couldn't speak as the Laird's warm breath brushed her ear, her mouth dry as a stone. Becoming the centre of every man's attention was nothing short of her worst nightmare. Over the roaring in her ears, she barely managed to understand it was not her they were looking for.

These were not Lord Ashburn's men.

The officers moved closer, one releasing his sword and gesturing with his other hand, never taking his eyes off the Laird. "Slide down off the horse, ma'am. We'll protect you from the heathen."

Duncan soothed his horse which, sensing the tension, had stepped sideways.

Heathen? Her own countrymen had shown their true colours, where the Laird had granted her shelter. He'd been honest in his dislike but still given her warmth and safety. He was no heathen.

"No." Frances stared down the officer and said in a clear, cold voice, "I am not being held against my will."

No one moved, and she swallowed again. "Thank you for your concern. Please, go about your business. I am fine."

"You heard the lady." Duncan nudged his horse and the officers had no choice but to move and give them passage.

They cantered away.

"Know those men do you, Miss Rothbury?" His voice was soft but there was no mistaking the menace in the heat of his breath.

"No, I do not."

The sick feeling in Frances' stomach would not go away. Particularly when she heard the dire mutterings of Laird's men, knowing despite his silence, he would be agreeing with them.

She wondered how long it would be until the Lord's men found her, and she faced a similar situation. Once they found her, though, there would be no reprieve. The Laird wouldn't be able to rescue her then. Frances couldn't help but feel her days were numbered.

CHAPTER THREE

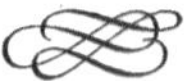

End of Spring, 1748

*D*uncan shifted and rolled over for what felt like the hundredth time. He couldn't sleep, blaming the full moon shining its silvery glow across his bed. "Tis the bloody moon, not the *Sassenach*," he grumbled to himself.

But it wasn't the moon occupying his thoughts. *She* was. Miss Rothbury. Disgusted with himself, he threw back the covers and sat on the edge of the bed, willing away the heat prowling beneath his skin. Maybe a book would distract him from thinking about the curve of her lush lips when she smiled. A rare enough event that had him staring at her like a lovesick youth when she did.

Scrubbing a hand over his face, he rose and then dressed. His solicitor in Edinburgh faithfully complied with his request to send books as they arrived. Consequently, he was stocking the library his father had never bothered with.

As he walked the hall, he didn't expect to see a strip of light emanating from under the library door. But before he even pushed it open, he knew who'd be in there. And damned himself for not even hesitating.

Her startled eyes immediately found his and she stood, folding her hands together. "L-Laird Grant..."

"Miss Rothbury."

For a moment, they both stared at one another before she picked up the book she'd been reading and closed it. "I'm sorry, I'll leave—"

"Stay. I granted you the permission to use the library whenever you wished." His gaze narrowed as the wariness in her expression increased. "I'm not about to toss you out."

Indecision was written all over her face and she kept sneaking looks at him. When she bit her lip, it had him hiding a sudden realisation she might possibly feel as he did. Something primitive he hadn't realised he'd kept so tightly leashed was let loose and it took a moment of firm resolve to immediately bring it to heel. He relished her dilemma; satisfied she might feel the same turmoil that plagued him.

She firmed her lips, and then gave a nod. "Thank you, Laird. I will stay for a little while."

He prowled over to the shelves, looking for the space that housed the book she was reading. Ah, Tobias Smollett. *The Adventures of Roderick Random. What do you think of it so far?"

She didn't answer immediately, and he glanced her way, seeing only her arm and hands due to the high-back chair.

"It certainly is an adventure, living up to its title."

"I've heard Smollett himself was in the Royal Navy and gives a realistic accounting of what it was like, despite it being a work of fiction."

"You haven't read it yet?" She peered around the high backing of the chair.

"No. It was only published this year. It arrived two days ago."

She rose and walked to him, holding out the

book. "I can't read your book when you haven't even had a chance to read it."

For a moment, he didn't move, then pushed the book back toward her, his hand half on hers. "Nay, Miss Rothbury, I'll not interrupt your reading. Once you start, you have to finish."

She pushed back, despite a becoming pink staining her cheeks. "But it's—"

"Nay. It's my book and I get to say who reads it."

Her hand fell away, and she dropped a small curtsey. "Thank you, Laird. Tis very generous of you."

She returned to her chair, leaving him standing there with his hand tingling. His fingers slowly curled into a fist, holding on to the sensation.

Turning back to the shelves he silently cursed the turmoil she caused him as he studied his books, seeing none of them. "You are having trouble sleeping, Miss Rothbury?"

"A little. The moon is bright tonight."

"Aye. The moon."

Restless, unable to choose a book after selecting a few before replacing them back on the shelf, Duncan stalked over to the cabinet and extracted a bottle of his father's finest whiskey. The old man rarely drank whiskey towards the end of his life, except for his wee drams of the finest he could get his hands on, when he could tolerate it. Snagging two glasses, he walked over to Frances and poured a finger in each before holding one out to her.

She looked up at him with wide blue eyes.

"It'll help you sleep." Nudging the glass into her hand, he sat in the chair next to hers with the small table between them.

"I…I don't normally drink whiskey."

"Take a sip and warm it on your tongue before swallowing."

She did as he bade but still coughed after her first

swallow, blowing out her breath with a tiny laugh. "Like fire," she gasped.

Duncan couldn't help but smile, and then laughed when she promptly took another sip.

"We'll make a Scots out of you yet," he chuckled.

The hint of a smile lingered, and she suddenly went from pretty to downright beautiful. Duncan subsided back into his chair, tossing back the whiskey in one hit. Unlike his father, he was not a big drinker, and winced, yet needed its bite.

He couldn't deny he admired Miss Rothbury, her calm, demure demeanour. He also couldn't deny his attraction to her.

It seemed everyone had fallen in love with his governess. Well, everyone except Malcolm. And that was the strangest thing. Malcolm, usually the protector, was adored by all women. Duncan remembered Mrs Cullen handing him extra coins the other day. *"The lass is giving me a portion of her wage back, Laird. Do you ken? She thinks she's using too many candles."*

"Miss Rothbury gave me her gloves because mine were so worn, Laird. She's an angel."

"The guv'ness read me the letter, Laird and then helped me to write one back. She be a good 'un."

"Miss Wotherbury rubbed my back last night cos I had a sore tummy, Papa. I like her."

Duncan looked at the bottom of his empty glass and contemplated more whiskey. He'd spent time with the English, he knew their culture. They viewed themselves as being elite, better than any other.

She was different. She did not assume because of where she was born, that she was better. She was quiet and humble, kept out of his way and looked after his children as though they were her own. Exactly as a governess should…and yet somehow *not*.

She was hiding something.

Clearly highborn, he would bet his horse, *Sterrm*,

that she was not what she made out to be—just a governess.

Two days ago, when the solicitor's factotum had delivered his books, Duncan had given him a letter of instruction to take back. He wanted answers to his questions about Miss Rothbury's life before she arrived on his doorstep. When the time was right, he would question her, but knew he wasn't going to get the answers he needed. She never spoke of her life with anyone, careful to give only general answers.

He took a deep breath, and stood, needing to leave before the restlessness in his blood made him do something he knew he'd regret. He looked down at her stubbornly bent head. "When you've finished *'The Adventures of Roderick Random'*, I recommend you read *'Pamela'*."

She rose and curtsied. "Thank you, I will."

Duncan placed his glass on the small table between them and walked to the door. With his hand on the knob, he stopped. "Goodnight Miss Rothbury. Sleep well."

"And you, Laird Grant. Goodnight."

Duncan closed the door behind him and ground his teeth. He knew he wasn't going to sleep a wink.

~

He was watching them again.

The tingle in her shoulder blades was a familiar experience and now not quite so daunting as her first weeks at Muckrach Castle.

Of course, she had no illusions he would be watching *her*. It was his children who captured his attention, their well-being of paramount importance, and Frances approved wholeheartedly. It was rare for a man of his station to display such an interest in his children.

Frances did not turn around but continued to walk the perimeter of the castle fence, watching as the children stretched their legs, playing in the warm sunshine. Brodie had climbed a tree and taunted his sister who could not reach the lowest branch.

"Remember what I told you Roslyn?"

Roslyn turned with a hopeful look. "Aye, Miss Wothbury. If I can't get down by myself, I shouldn't climb it in the first place."

"Will you be able to get down?"

"Aye!"

"She won't Miss—!"

"Brodie."

The quiet authority of her voice stilled his instantly. With a resigned sigh, he clambered down to help boost his sister up on the lowest branch.

"Remember Roslyn, you'll be getting down by yourself."

"Aye, Miss!"

A movement from the corner of her eye caught her attention and she watched as the Laird strode across the grounds toward her, ignoring the leap in her blood. How many times had she reminded herself that she was a wanted fugitive? And even despite that, also a monster? *He was not for her.*

Folding her hands in front, she schooled her features to bland interest and waited.

"Good afternoon, Laird Grant." She dipped a curtsy.

"Miss Rothbury." It was their ritual, now. He stood beside her, a large man of compelling masculinity as they watched the children bicker and play in the shade of a spreading oak.

"You are teaching Brodie archery."

"Yes. He is a natural, with good strength and an eye for aiming true."

The ensuing silence did not bother her anymore. She was well-used to his silences.

"And you're teaching Roslyn?"

"Yes. She should learn, just as her brother does."

Another silence. Frances waited, watching the children.

"Did you enjoy 'Pamela'?"

Startled, Frances looked up at him then looked ahead and straightened her shoulders. *He'd noticed.* "It was an interesting read."

"What did you think of Mr B's character?"

"You've read it?"

He nodded, his eyes on the children.

For a moment, Frances couldn't answer. Trust him to home in on exactly the character who caused her the most consternation. Looking up at him, she finally answered in an emotionless tone, "I found his character to be without principles."

He nodded slowly. "Aye, English lords." It was said with some rancour and Frances did not, could not blame him.

"You surprise me, Miss Rothbury."

"Oh?"

"I would have thought the romance would appeal to you, especially his redemption in asking for Pamela's hand. Who could resist an English Lord?"

Frances couldn't help her cold tone. "It is a work of fiction; the author shines too kind a light on the Lord. Reality is a different kettle of fish."

"Aye, a man in his position would think nothing of using Pamela for his own end."

"Yes. Particularly after doing everything in his power to proposition and ruin her."

"I believe we're in accord, Miss Rothbury. The notion of a Lord offering his hand in marriage to a young maidservant is as substantial and tangible as smoke from a dry fire."

Frances nodded, screening her eyes with her lashes, unable to help the tightening of her lips. He was right. Her own terrifying experience with an English Lord proved very different from fiction. The silence grew, and, because he made no move to leave, she decided to tackle an issue plaguing her for months.

"I am using more candles than necessary, Laird Grant." Every night since he'd plucked her from the village church, extra candles appeared in her room, replacing the burned-down one from the previous night.

"I'm not aware of any burden on my expenditure, Miss Rothbury."

"Regardless of your say-so, I have taken the liberty of reimbursing Mrs Cullen. I'm sure the housekeeper can use the extra."

He looked down at her with a shuttered expression.

Frances raised her chin, amplifying the confidence in her tone, trying not to notice the breadth of his shoulders, the way his rolled up shirt sleeves showed the tan skin of his forearms.

One brow rose. "Mrs Cullen has already reported to me, handing over the extra. Your wage remains the same, Miss Rothbury, regardless of your machinations."

Despite his forbidding tone, she pressed on, "I don't need more—"

Roslyn's high-pitched cry sounded an alarm, and they both looked up. The child was stuck in the tree on the low branch, wanting to follow Brodie.

"Brodie! I can't get down! Papa!"

The Laird took a step.

Instantly, Frances clamped a hand around his forearm. "Stop."

He looked down at her small hand clutching his arm.

She felt the hard muscles flex beneath her fingers and couldn't stop the soft warmth that swept into her cheeks.

"Beg your pardon, Laird. She needs to learn to get down herself," she said in a low voice, removing her hand and striding forward. "Come Roslyn, what did you tell me before Brodie helped you up the tree?"

"I don't care! Papa, come get me down."

The Laird did not move at the petulant summons, only to call out in his deep voice, "I distinctly heard you tell Miss Rothbury you could get down, Roslyn."

After a tantrum, a few tears and some coaching for the placement of feet, she slid down by herself, her small face glowing with achievement. "I did it! Papa, I did it! Brodie, did you see me?"

She scampered after her brother, who gave her gruff praise and then pushed her over in a mock fight.

Frances smiled and continued to follow the children down the path around the castle walls to the next large tree to climb. Aware of the Laird following, she hid her surprise and her smile faded. Normally, their interaction would have ended.

Her intuition working overtime, this silence had an expectant quality she did not like. She quickened her step, but he matched her pace with ease, drawing alongside her.

"Tell me, Miss Rothbury, what is your reason for tying yourself to your bed?"

Frances stopped dead, her wide eyes flying to his. "How did…you've been in my room?" she demanded, her cheeks blazing with agitated heat. "I…Such liberties are unacceptable—"

His expression gave nothing away. "Calm yourself. The first night you stayed, you cried out and I came in when you didn't reply to my enquiry on your health."

She tried to breathe through her undiluted horror.

"And no, naught since then," he stated. "But I've heard you cry out on other nights since."

A tense silence stretched between them.

"You didn't answer my question, Miss Rothbury."

"I…the children require my attention. Brodie, stop pulling your sister's pigtails!" she called out, walking away from him, uncaring if he wasn't fooled by her ruse of watching the children.

In three large strides, the Laird caught her arm. She had no choice but to stop. "Oh!" she squeaked, and then cleared her throat, saying in a firmer voice, "Please, Laird. Take your hand off me."

The warm hand dropped away, but before relief could emerge, he stepped in front of her, effectively cutting her off from the children.

Frances inhaled, alarmed when her breath hitched. His gaze narrowed ever so slightly in a look she was coming to recognise.

He wasn't going to stop until he had answers.

"I have many questions, Miss Rothbury. Your answers are required."

Tension screwed the nerves in her overwrought stomach into knots. Gritting her teeth with reluctance, she answered with ill-grace, trying to tamp down her fear. "Yes."

"Yes, you still tie yourself to the bed?"

Her lips tightened, "Yes."

"Why?"

Taking in a deep breath, she answered, "I sleepwalk. Or rather, not so long as I am tied. Your questions…your questions are unseemly. I should be…the children—"

"Are playing. I understand now."

Trepidation tightened her throat. She'd done her best to keep out of his way. Since the night he'd brought her back to Muckrach Castle, she'd attended to the children and squirreled herself away, out of his sight. Obviously not as well as she'd thought.

"Your fear of the dark and your sleepwalking, I think, go hand in hand. I had thought extra candles would alleviate some of that."

Frances had had enough. She'd answered his questions, now she was done. "My problems are my own, Laird Grant."

"Your problems could impact my children."

"They do not," she answered back immediately, stung.

"You sleep during the day, if you can."

Horrified at just how much he'd watched her activities, she snapped, "I *never* sleep when I'm looking after the children."

"I know, but you still sleep during your allotted time off. After your walk, of course."

"That is my prerogative, Laird!"

"Agreed, Miss Rothbury." Frustration filled his tone. "However, it's your dreams I'm interested in. Murder and Lords? What past are you escaping?"

Aghast, Frances stepped back, feeling the first burn of frost rippling around her heart as her *berserker* rose at the perceived threat. She tripped on an unexpected tuft of grass on the pathway and turned her ankle, flailing for less than a moment. The Laird reached out and grasped her by the upper arms, righting her until she found her footing.

Conscious of his proximity, she froze. His hands were holding her with a firm, warm grip in the cool shade beneath the tree. She could smell his clean scent. He was so male, so foreign, so *large*.

And then the frost melted, as it had the day down at the river. How could this be? How was it that her *berserker* waned when with all other men, it roared out of control? All she could do was try to breathe; her gaze captured by his.

His eyes were alit with a grave curiosity as he repeated softly, "What past are you escaping?"

Frances could only stare at him as she desperately tried to maintain her composure. The man had a mind like a steel trap and the patience of a predator. When she'd thought he was watching the children, he'd also been watching her.

She'd seen a picture of a wolf once. With his light coloured eyes and dark brown hair, right at this moment, he reminded her of it.

Summoning a smile to her frozen lips, she brazened. "Let me go, please."

The half-smile that quirked his lips did not reach his eyes. And he did not let go.

"I am alright. I can stand on my own feet." She lowered her lashes to escape the intensity of his gaze and tugged gently against his restraining hands. "Thank you, Laird Grant."

He slowly let go of her arms. She took a deep breath, wishing he would also step back. She could still feel the imprint of his warm hands on her arms. And feel a stirring low down in her belly that was different to the *berserker*. She immediately tamped it down, but it had mind of its own, pulsating not with ice, but heat.

"Repeated night terrors in any sleep indicate a problem."

Her gaze met his. "You doubt my care of your children?"

"No. As a governess you are exemplary. Roslyn has gained confidence." He looked towards his children.

The relief that her position would not be terminated made her feel dizzy and she blinked rapidly.

He glanced back at her. "She too, suffers night-mares which have lessened. I put it down to your warmth with her."

"She has a beautiful nature and is easy to love." Frances stepped sideways, relieved at the change in subject and grateful for the opening to remove herself from his presence.

"Good day to you, Laird." She walked on, acting as though nothing had happened, that his touch, his proximity had stirred sensations in her that were best buried.

His soft, "Aye, good day to you, Miss Rothbury," behind her had the hairs on her nape stirring.

He watched her still.

She bit her lip, allowing herself, just for a moment, to remember that day down near the river when his naked body had pressed against hers. She inhaled as she increased her pace to catch up with the children.

What would it have been like...?

No.

A hundred times no.

That way lay a disaster of epic proportions. He was not for her. At any given moment, Lord Ashburn's men could ride into the grounds of Muckrach Castle and take her prisoner. Nobody could stop them.

Except her.

She was living a lie.

Giving herself a shake, she smiled as Brodie called out to her, deliberately tamping down those memories. But from then on, Frances couldn't help feeling hunted right down to her toes.

CHAPTER FOUR

Fall 1748

"I see you've finished 'Beauty and the Beast'."

A small smile stretched her lips as the Laird sat next to her in the dining hall. It was Sunday morning of her day off and she'd risen late after reading well into the night. This morning, she'd replaced the book in the library.

Since that night in the library, and especially the day he'd asked about her sleep walking, she'd done her best never to accidentally run into him.

"Yes."

"What did you think?"

She chose her words carefully as she glanced at him. "It's beautifully written."

"Oh?" He caught her gaze. "You didn't like it?"

"I liked it very much," she nodded. "Have you read it?"

A nod and a twist of his lips produced a cynical smile. "Aye, man, ever the beast."

Frances screened her eyes with lashes. *No, not always man.* She did not want to tell him the truth— that she was the beast. In her eyes, he was the beauty. An honourable man, untainted by the base instinct to kill, a mindless beast. A fair man, able to use reason, always. Fair on the eyes, too.

"And the woman, soothing his savage breast. Soft, romantic notions."

"Yes, all for the romance. It is what society would have us think and act." She forced another smile. "'Tis the way of the world, is it not?"

"That women can't be beast-like? I disagree. I've met a few beastly ladies in my time."

The words spilled out before she could stop them. "What was the Beast always reminding Beauty? 'Do not trust too much to your eyes'. Yes, women can definitely be beast-like."

He frowned and went to speak but she forestalled him with a quick smile to diffuse the tension she'd created. "We are just quieter, and smaller with less…hair."

He chuckled, a pleasing deep sound, his eyes crinkling attractively.

Frances had to look away, the ache in her heart harder and harder to bear. Her gaze clashed with Malcolm's, sitting further up the hall and her smile died.

The man did not hide his dislike.

At every opportunity, he reminded her with just such a dark look that she was on borrowed time, that her place at the castle was not permanent and tenuous at best. That any day the Lord's men could find her and renounce her position. Take her away from the warmth and safety she'd come to cherish.

Lowering her lashes, Frances quietly despaired for Malcolm. The murder of his sister had been appalling tale, one Mrs Cullen had told with tears in her eyes. Frances finally understood his hatred.

For it was widely believed that English deserters committed the shocking atrocity. *Her own countrymen.*

Frances could not hold any antipathy toward Malcolm. Not only had he lost his sister to violence, but his entire family, wiped out by scarlet fever when he was only a young boy.

He was alone in the world, with the Laird his only anchor.

Like her own brother, Malcolm had been his sister's protector, alone against a cruel world. Frances knew the anger and pain would hide a large reservoir of guilt and despair. And the sense he'd failed.

No one could help him with that.

"Are you hiding in plain sight then, Miss Rothbury?"

Recalled to the conversation, Frances stiffened at the question. She curled her fingers into her palms beneath the table. *Little did he know.*

Forcing a smile, she answered as best she could. "I'm just a governess, Laird."

Some emotion flashed in his eyes, so fleeting she wondered if she'd really seen it.

Looking away, she rallied. "Where are the children, today?" Frances put herself firmly back on track.

"Mrs Cullen has them. I've already warned them both to leave you alone on your day off."

"It's alright. They're no bother. I might take them on my walk later this afternoon."

"Leave them, enjoy your solitude, although do not wander from the castle grounds. Fergus advises you've been wandering farther and farther a-field."

At his comment she frowned. "Fergus has been watching me?"

He took in a breath and hesitated, as though weighing up whether to speak. "I set a watch for the safety of everyone. Deserters still roam, Miss Rothbury, a little too close for my liking. It may be best to shorten your walk time. Winter will soon take your walks from you, albeit."

As usual, he was observant, knowing she loved the hours she spent walking along the river and in the forest. The peace was indescribable. On her walks, she could almost imagine she was normal. The monster had been quiet, of late.

Maybe in this place, she *could* be normal. The idea was so tempting, she almost dared hope.

"That's a pensive look, Miss Rothbury. Something be amiss?" His gaze narrowed, "Have you seen these men?"

She glanced up at him. "No, of course not. Nothing is amiss, Laird. Good day to you." Standing, it was her turn to look down at him, not flinching from his searching gaze. Dropping a small curtsey, she turned and left.

*H*ours later, Frances approached the entry way to the castle, calling out a greeting to Gill on his way back from town to his crofter's cottage. It was getting on towards late afternoon and she tugged her jacket together against the chill.

The Laird was right, winter was fast approaching—

A child's shrill scream rent the air, and then the sounds of shouting. Frances inhaled sharply then picked up her skirts and started running.

Was that Brodie?

The screams continued as she neared the kitchen entrance and darted inside.

Her heart thundering, she saw the Laird, his voice booming out in a vicious tirade, holding Brodie face down on the floor and ripping at his shirt.

Frances stiffened, heaving in a shocked breath. Surely the Laird couldn't—

The Laird bellowed again, and Brodie screamed as the shirt was ripped off his back.

"No," she moaned in disbelief. But her eyes saw what they saw.

Frost filled her veins, the *berserker* rising so fast she had no hope of controlling it. Gasping as the freeze turned her heart to ice, she tried in vain to use her rationale. Her fingers clenched into a fist as she advanced towards the Laird. But part of her was silently screaming in revulsion.

She couldn't kill him!

It was then she saw the smoke and the last of the flame being tamped out of the shirt by one of the men.

Halting, Frances immediately screened her eyes with her lashes. Grinding her teeth, it took effort to prevent the killing rage from taking over. His father wasn't abusing the boy, he'd been trying to *save* him.

Oh, God. She'd been on the verge of killing an innocent man!

A small sob escaped her dry mouth and she kept her lashes down, grappling with the horror.

From the edge of her vision, Brodie writhed on the floor, clearly in pain. And it was his pain that helped to subdue the *berserker*. It waned almost instantly. She took a step, halting again when someone blocked her path.

"This isn't your concern, Miss Rothbury. Stay away."

Malcolm.

She dared not look up at the Laird's man for she knew her eyes would surely give her away. The urge to help Brodie was strong, in turn feeding the tendrils of *berserker* still swirling.

Biting off each word, she said, "Excuse me, Mr Tulloch. I am his governess and I have just as much right as anyone who cares for the lad."

"'Tis none of your business. Stand aside." He'd planted his feet apart and was not going to move.

Frances felt her eyes narrow and before she could stop herself, shoved Malcolm out of the way, uncaring of using the strength of a man to do so. She flicked him a glance and saw that he reeled, taking several backward steps before the backs of his knees hit the long seat and he sat abruptly, astonishment on his face. She couldn't blame him; he was as tall and as broad as Duncan. A normal woman would have no hope of moving him.

Tearing her narrowed gaze away from him, she screened her eyes as she ordered, "Water. Get a pan of water, the coldest you can get it!"

"Aye, water!" The Laird seconded her call, his voice hoarse.

She kept her eyes on Brodie, not trusting herself to look at the Laird. She scanned the boy who had subsided into whimpers through his clenched teeth.

"Where else is he burned?"

"Just his arm."

"Papa, it hurts," Brodie cried.

Frances stroked his hair as the pan of water was brought to his side. She pushed his arm into it, and he cried out again as the cold water shocked his arm. After a minute, his clenched muscles relaxed a little, and he took a deep, shuddering breath.

"Better?" she asked, scanning his face with anxious eyes.

"Aye," he sighed, tears streaking his cheeks. "Sorry Papa. I'm sorry."

"Hush, boy. I think you've punishment enough." The Laird's deep voice was soft as he cradled his child's head.

"Master Brodie, how many times have I told you to stay away from the ovens?" Mrs Cullen's shrill voice sounded over their heads and then Frances heard a sob from the older woman.

"Hush now, Mrs Cullen this is no fault of yours. The boy will live, and no doubt never go near the ovens again. Is that right Brodie?"

"Aye, Papa. Never. I'm sorry Mrs Cullen." His eyes filled with tears again, despite his attempts to stem them.

Now that the initial shock had passed, Frances could hear the shaken murmurs and the sound of crying. Roslyn had seen the whole thing. Frances saw the child, her fingers in her mouth, her face streaked with tears and beckoned her over.

Roslyn flew over to Frances and buried her face in her neck. "It's alright little sparrow, Brodie is alright, see?"

They all looked at Brodie's arm where a large chunk of ember had burned through his shirt and sizzled his skin. Already, large blisters were forming. She looked at the Laird. "Do you have a healer, someone who knows herbs?"

The Laird nodded, then turned to one of his men, issuing orders. Brodie took his arm out of the water and then immediately dropped it back in again, a shiver shaking his frame.

Frances told him, "Don't take it out, young man. Mrs Cullen, can you organise a pitcher of water to be brought, we need to keep the water as cold as possible."

Mrs Cullen bustled off, the gratefulness for the chore written all over her face.

"Without your quick action Laird, he would have been burned far worse." Frances kept her voice low as she soothed Roslyn, who had buried her face in Frances' neck again, stroking her hair.

She felt, rather than saw the Laird's glance.

"Miss Wothbury, will he be alright?"

Roslyn's voice was soft, only for her ears. Frances hugged her tight for a moment and drew her away from Brodie, leaving him with his father. "He will be fine, little sparrow. Will you help look after him?"

"Yes, I will." She hiccupped and settled more fully against Frances. "I saw your face, Miss Wotherbury. You looked scary and your eyes seemed to burn like fire, only they were blue."

Every muscle in Frances' body locked in total panic. *The child had seen her nearly change?* It hurt to breathe, and she could only take shallow breaths. Trying to speak normally, she said, "It might have seemed like that, darling. Everyone was upset."

Roslyn pulled away for a moment and looked at her. "No, Miss Wotherbury. I saw it. Then you covered your eyes with your eyelids before Malcolm stopped you." She touched a soft finger to Frances' eyelid. "And now they are the same as they usually are."

Roslyn hugged her again, seeking comfort. Frances' thoughts whirled. She wanted desperately to seek the sanctuary of her room. Unable to bear the thought of scaring the girl so much, she would lose their love and she would have to leave. Oh, God. *She could have killed their father!*

The little arms tightened, as though Roslyn sensed her turmoil. Helpless, Frances rubbed her back, her heart breaking.

"Don't ever leave us, Miss Wotherbury."

Frances closed her eyes. It was looking more and more like she would have to. She was a beast. A monster. If Roslyn saw her as full *berserker*, she would never recover. *Oh, God.*

The thought of leaving…her heartbeat stumbled as her heart contracted, the little pain causing her to gasp softly. She didn't want to leave. She had to protect her secret. But more importantly, the people around her.

The children came first, because she loved them. She would see Brodie through the worst of his injury and then…then she would have to leave. Her arms tightened around Roslyn, the ache in her chest immense.

In due course, the healer was brought to the castle, an older woman who was greeted with a reverence she seemed to shrug off. Her gaze sharpened when she was introduced to Frances, but without saying anything, she turned to Brodie and clicked her tongue.

They lay him on the table, and she produced bandages dipped in fat and honey and wrapped the boy's arm until it was thick and sealed. She spoke in Gaelic the whole time, sometimes humming. Frances found her eyes closing at one point, the woman's voice so soothing and melodic.

Brodie drifted off to sleep and a sense of peace pervaded the kitchen after the tumult, everyone slowly returning to their duties. The Laird gathered the boy up and took him to the sleep chamber he shared with Roslyn, while Mrs Cullen bade the healer to stay for the evening meal.

Only once did Frances catch Malcolm's gaze, the speculative distrust like a warning. To avoid him, she then took Roslyn off to her bed, staying a while with her until she drifted off to sleep. She checked on Brodie, who was sleeping soundly.

As she watched both of her charges faces in the flickering candlelight, she rubbed her forehead. She'd gone and done the very thing she should have avoided.

She loved them.

Destined never to have children of her own, Brodie and Roslyn were the closest thing to children she would ever have. She could never conceive of telling anyone about the dark secret of her *berserker*. And then there were the Lord's men. It was a miracle she hadn't yet been found.

She would have to leave soon. But where would she go? For her, there was nowhere else *to* go.

Burying her face in her hands, she tried to inhale to ease the ache in her heart. She then lowered her hands and sat straight. The *berserker* had risen, but she'd managed this time to control it before it took over.

She watched as her fingers curled into a fist, her resolve rising. The vile thing inside her must never be allowed out in this place. She could do it, there was no danger here, the Laird had adequate protections set in place.

She would stay until Brodie had recovered.

Her decision made, she felt a little better. Taking the first proper breath since she'd come back from her walk, Frances kissed each sleeping face and tucked the covers around them before seeking her own bed.

Frances woke and her eyes flew open. It was still dark, and she knew it would be hours before dawn. Unsure of what had woken her, she lay still for a moment, listening for a sound. A candle was still burning, its flickering light welcome in the darkness. The wind had risen during the night and was now whistling and moaning around the stone walls of the castle.

A faint sound caught her attention and she strained her ears.

Brodie. It sounded like the lad was calling out. Rising, she untied her wrist, wrapped her robe about her and picked up the candle, holding it aloft as she negotiated the passage to the children's room.

As she entered, she saw Roslyn was still fast asleep. Brodie was awake, holding his arm.

"Master Brodie, does it hurt?" she whispered, hurrying over.

"Aye, it's hurting." His normally stoic voice wobbled.

"I heard you call out."

He frowned. "Nay, Miss Rothbury, I dinna call out."

"Oh," she said, and then settled next to him, "I could have sworn I heard you call out. No matter, Mrs Cullen told me the healer said to keep the bandages on for nine days."

He straightened him arm, then brought it back to cradle. "It stings. It woke me up."

"I would think it would hurt." She looked kindly at him for a moment, then said, "Move over."

For a moment he just stared at her, then wriggled over on the bed. She slid further down against the pillow and gathered the blankets over her legs. Before he could say anything, she put her arm beneath his head and settled him against her shoulder.

He was stiff against her warmth.

"I'll tell you the story of David and Goliath. Do you know it?"

He shook his head and Frances settled into the soft pillows.

"Goliath was a giant. He was so big that his head seemed to brush the clouds…"

Her soft voice worked its magic and soon Brodie's head was resting against her, distracted from his pain by the story of the giant killer. She then heard his steady breathing and his body slumped against her. For a moment, she lay there, savouring his weight, until with a soft sigh, she knew she had to seek her own bed.

After rising and adjusting the blankets, she smoothed the edges as she looked down at his slumbering face. Her heart contracted. Bending, she pressed a whisper of a kiss on his forehead, something she'd never subject him to if he was awake.

He'd be in pain for a while, but she would do her best to help him through it.

Smothering a yawn, she turned, but her hand went to her chest in fright when she saw a large form in the partially open doorway.

The Laird.

Ignoring the skip in her heartbeat, she inhaled. Her previous fatigue disappeared, and everything came into sharp focus.

"Shhh," he bade and motioned her out into the hall.

Thankful he'd lit the torch, she quietly shut the door. It was when she turned, she became acutely conscious of her hair trailing down her back in a loose plait. "Laird Grant, I hope I didn't wake you?"

"Nay, I came to check on Brodie some time ago, but was entranced by your storytelling."

"His arm was hurting, I heard him cry out."

The Laird nodded, his grey eyes gleaming in the torch light. "You are good with him."

Averting her gaze, Frances tried to ignore the warmth his compliment gave her. "Thank you. He is a remarkable young boy, intelligent and strong. He's getting to the age where he will join you soon, to learn about his heritage."

At his silence, she glanced up and forced a smile. The awareness between them deepened and she found it hard to inhale a normal breath. Used to the chill in her blood, the heat prowling along her veins had her breathing in shallow spurts, and she moistened her dry lips as she stammered, "T-The hour is late, good night, Laird."

"Come, you've no candle. I'll walk you to your room."

"That is not nec…" Frances was left looking at the Laird's broad shoulders retreating down the hall, taking the light with him. Tightening her lips, she gathered the skirts of her robe and tried not to scurry after him as the dark nipped at her heels.

At her door, he placed the torch in the sconce and turned to her. Frances couldn't help but feel trapped in his gaze. The cold air between them seem to tighten, trying to draw her closer.

The Laird pulled something from his pocket. "Here."

She looked down at the candle in his large hand, and then back up at him.

He explained softly, "I thought a spare would be needed."

She swallowed, her heart expanding in her chest, and wrenched her gaze to the candle in his hand lest he see the emotion in her eyes. She raised tentative fingers, trying to avoid touching him. If she touched him…no, she couldn't.

She took the candle between her thumb and forefinger, and quickly lowered her hand, hardly daring to breathe. "Thank you, Laird Grant."

It didn't matter. He took the step to bring him closer, close enough for her to feel the warmth coming off his body in the chill of the night. The sound of the wind seemed far away, and her hand clenched around the candle as she fought the urge to move closer.

The gentle caress of his slightly rough fingers on her jaw had her gaze flying to his, watching the way the light from the torch gilded the stubble of his new beard and outlined his lips.

"Ever since our first meeting down at the river, I've wondered if your skin was as soft as it felt."

Frances tried to draw the air into her lungs, but her lungs refused to obey.

He cupped her jaw, running a thumb along her chin.

"Laird Gra—"

"Duncan, lass." He tilted her chin with the crook of his finger and his head bent, his thumb stroking the contours of her lips. They felt full, as though her blood loved his caress and followed it with mindless devotion.

He stopped, a breath away.

And Frances, mesmerised by the heat in his gaze, leaned in.

Soft lips touched hers for the briefest moment, and her heart shuddered to a stand-still.

"When you're going to kiss a man, you call him by his name." He whispered against her lips.

Her lashes, too heavy to hold up, fell. For the first time in the longest time, the darkness felt warm and safe as he pressed his mouth to hers once more.

His lips moved slowly over hers, learning their shape, nibbling here and there, while his hand cupped her cheek. When he withdrew, she followed his mouth with her own, raising up on tip toes.

His thumb swept over her bottom lip and then gently tugged.

Once more his mouth covered hers, except now Frances tasted him as his tongue gently licked inside. Her breath caught and then she exhaled as his tongue withdrew. Her hand came up, fingers wrapped around his arm to bolster herself as she tried to follow again, her senses registering the hard muscle.

"More, lass?" It was a low growl that raised goose-bumps on her skin.

Oh, yes.

Without hesitating, her lips parted, wanting only the pleasurable intimacy of his mouth on hers.

His hand shifted, sliding around her nape, burrowing into her loose plait. His lips touched hers and his tongue pushed slowly into her mouth. Shivering, Frances angled her head and touched her tongue to his, lost in the dark intimacy.

He made a deep sound in his throat as he thrust his tongue against hers, again and again. In a heartbeat, a heated pleasure turned the warmth in her blood to a raging inferno. Lost, she had no recollection when the Laird pushed her against the wall, wrapping a strong arm around her, his hand tightening in her hair. No recollection either, of her arms around his neck, wanting only to get closer, the voracious heat of his mouth delicious.

When his mouth left hers, she inhaled with greedy pulls of her lungs, only to lose her breath again when his lips travelled along the length of her jaw and then beneath, his new beard softly scraping her skin. He gently bit the sensitive skin along the tendon, and she gave a soft cry when the muscles deep in her pelvis contracted, her nails digging into his skin.

"Aye, lass, open your eyes. I need to see them."

She didn't understand the demand and he drew her head back. "Open your eyes, Frances."

Lifting her lashes, she wondered how such a simple action could be so hard.

"Aye," he breathed, "Blue eyes that blaze like a pure blue flame."

For a moment, she could only gaze at him, seeing the heat in his eyes, and then the words registered. She blinked, and her eyes stretched wide as horror replaced her desire. "No," she breathed.

"Frances?"

With a little gasp, she yanked her arms from

around his neck, trying to shrink back into the wall. Mentally flaying herself, she shut her traitorous mouth and pushed against his broad chest. He stepped back, the warmth of his hand falling away from her nape.

A frown darkened his brow. "Frances? What's amiss? Have I hurt you?" he demanded.

Yes, he'd hurt her, her heart ached unbearably. For he was not for her...

Taking a moment, she swallowed and shook her head. "No. No you haven't." Then said quietly. "Please address me as Miss Rothbury, Laird."

His grey gaze narrowed, and she looked away, unable to meet his eyes. She'd never let anyone so physically close to her. The loss of the warmth of his body was not just physical, and she struggled with the turmoil of her emotions.

She swallowed again. "My behaviour was…" She floundered, unable to find the right word.

He remained silent, offering no help.

"Unseemly. I…it won't happen again."

A muscle flexed in his jaw.

The silence between them expanded until Frances wanted to scream. She decided it was past time to seek the sanctuary of her room and stepped sideways, saying with careful politeness, "Thank you for the candle—"

"Dinna move."

She froze, skewered by his sharp gaze.

"We just kissed. And it fair burned my socks off."

Composing her expression, Frances retreated within herself, as she'd done countless times in the past. Although she'd never been kissed before, she did the only thing she knew best, brushing it under the carpet. Pretend those soul-stirring moments had never happened.

How could she? They were seared into her brain...

"Laird Grant. Tonight was…was an aberration. Silly things happen in the dark of early morning—"

"Your mouth was on mine."

She drew in a deep breath through her nose. "Nothing really hap—"

"Your tongue thrust against mine." Brutally candid, he spared her nothing.

Her lips tightened as heat crawled into her cheeks.

He took a step.

And Frances immediately held up her hand to ward him off. "No."

He couldn't know what little will left she had to resist him if he kissed her again.

The silence reigned again, holding its breath as the air between them became a battle ground for their will. The determination in his gaze was relentless.

Somehow, she found the tatters of her composure. "No. I won't acknowledge what happened. Because it will *never* happen again. I am in your employ. That. Is. All."

Frances met his determined gaze head on with her own. "You are not the first to try."

His brows snapped together.

"Nor will you likely be the last," she added in a quiet voice.

With that, she stepped sideways to her door, closing it gently behind her. Her shoulders slumped, and she struggled to breathe as despair cramped her lungs. Just like she had with the children, she'd gone and done something immensely, and utterly stupid.

At what point had she fallen in love with a man she could never have?

CHAPTER FIVE

Mid Fall 1748

"But we aren't allowed to, Miss Wothbury!"

"Rothbury, sparrow," Frances automatically corrected. She forged a determined path toward the northern field where the archery targets stood, basking in the weak afternoon sun. The large clearing was the perfect space for archery, surrounded by the woods on all sides. It was just warm enough to continue the outdoor activity.

Brodie led the way, eager to move after his forced inactivity. "It's alright, Roslyn. Da told us we weren't to go to the northern field by ourselves. Miss Rothbury is with us."

"Oh." Roslyn frowned and then gasped Frances' hand, apparently mollified.

Frances was grateful for the reprieve in the weather for it had rained and grown colder in the four weeks since Brodie had burned his arm. In truth, she was grateful to escape the walls of the castle…and the Laird.

Because he was the Laird. Not Duncan.

As she bade him, he'd kept away from her, barely offering a greeting. But his gaze on her was like the sleet that had lashed the castle for two days; icy and relentless. She'd avoided meeting his eyes unless necessary.

Even to the point that others in the castle had noticed, including Mrs Cullen, her small eyes darting between Frances and Laird when they were unable to avoid each other at mealtimes.

There was no stirring discussion about books. No anything.

The only one happy about it was Malcolm. He'd even greeted her the other morning, despite its curtness.

Her lips tightening, Frances straightened from adjusting Brodie's fingers and stance. Pensive, she turned her eyes on the target. Only in the darkness of night would she admit to missing the Laird's conversation, his easy smile, how the air between them would sparkle like a summer afternoon when they discussed a character from a book, or the children. *And his lips on hers. The heat from his warm, hard body, his mouth...oh, the dark magic of his mouth making her forget everything but the sensations it evoked in her body.*

Shaking her head, she blinked away her sudden tears, cross with herself. She couldn't trust herself not to hurt him. His children. His people. She tried to imagine telling him what she was. Every single time, the words would not come. How could they? Even if they did, he would recoil in horror and denounce her for the monster she was.

She watched Brodie as he lined up the target and let the arrow fly true. He was much better. In fact, he was fully healed. And yet she was still at Muckrach Castle. By now, she should have taken her leave. It *had* to be soon.

"It's better this way." She whispered the words, letting the breeze take them.

The children spent an hour practicing archery

and soaking up the feeble afternoon sun, until a chill wind eddied around them and the shadows of the surrounding wood lengthened.

"Come Brodie, enough for the day."

"Just one more shot!" he called.

Frances shook her head, "No, we must head back now—"

"Miss Wothbury, who are they?"

Frances looked down at Roslyn, then in the direction she was pointing and frowned.

Two men ambled their horses along the fringes of the wood across the other side of the field, their red coats faded but unmistakable. She dared not move, hoping they would not see her and the children.

Uneasy, she watched them as the muscles in her stomach tightened. When they headed their horses toward her and the children, she stiffened, the uneasy feeling intensifying, like lightning running along her stretched nerves.

As they neared, she recognised the menacing brutes from the evening the Laird had taken her back to the castle. Especially the leering one, Rob. On an indrawn breath, panic clutched her stomach. She looked behind her, measuring the distance to the safety of the wood.

She had no hope of outrunning two men on horseback. Not with the children.

"Brodie," she said softly, not taking her eyes of the men for a second. "Take your sister's hand."

Brodie dropped his bow. He reached for his sister.

As the horses cantered closer, one of the men nudged the other. The direction of his intention was plain from the look in his eye and the insolent, cruel smile on his face.

Ice surged into her blood from one heartbeat to the next. She looked down as the metallic taste flooded her mouth.

"Run for the wood. Climb the tallest tree you can find. Help your sister. I'll be right behind you."

"But—"

"Go Brodie!" She pushed him with ungentle hands. "And when you're safe, look away and cover your sister's eyes. Promise me!" she snarled through gritted teeth.

Brodie did as she bade, stuttering a promise and dragging Roslyn behind him at a dead run.

Breathing hard, Frances turned her gaze back to the men who were coming fast, their faded red coats spread out like demon's wings. She struggled against the *berserker* rising, trying to hold the ice accumulating in her blood at bay.

But as they neared, she saw the eyes of the one shearing off, heading toward the children, the promise of violence in his eyes.

"Get the brats, Rob!" the other one called, "You'll get your turn later."

Everything seemed to slow as she catalogued Rob's features in detail; the grimy kerchief about his neck, the sag in his unshaven jowls, the dirt beneath his fingernails, the once broken nose and the scar that bisected his eyebrow.

The viciousness in his expression as he looked at the children.

Her teeth ached from the ice in her blood and for the first time in her life she welcomed it's burn. She let the rage come, overwhelmed by the need to let it out, her fingers tensing into claws. Her breath misted as she breathed out through clenched teeth.

Grown men preying on those smaller and physically weaker than themselves.

Bastards.

No more.

"No more," she snarled.

No one would harm her children, *ever*.

Drawing in a breath, her gaze narrowed, and vengeance soared. One moment she'd started to run towards the children, a chilling, primal scream erupting from her mouth, and the next, the world stopped as the Berserker rage struck like an icy lightning bolt and took over.

~

As soon as Duncan saw the stable boy galloping toward him, he knew something was wrong. He dropped the log he was working into position for the new fence, and straightened, his eyes narrowing against the afternoon sun.

"Deserters!"

The hair on his neck lifted at the boy's cry.

"Deserters, Laird! In the northern field," the boy cried as the horse skidded to halt, "Miss Rothbury and your bairns—"

His heart stopped, and then raced. He leapt onto his horse, spitting a vile curse and wheeled the stallion into a gallop with gritted teeth. The nightmare rose to choke his breath as he raced through the forest, finding the shortest route.

Within moments that felt like aeons, he burst through the trees from the south, overtaking the half dozen men running toward the archery targets. He searched the field for deserters but inexplicably found only a riderless horse that shied away from him as he pulled the stallion up short.

His heart in his mouth, he wheeled his horse around again, yet only sound he could hear the frantic, pounding beat of his heart.

Suddenly, a high-pitched, muffled scream came from the bank of trees to his right.

Duncan spurred his stallion toward the sound.

It was dim in the wood, golden slants of afternoon sunshine slicing through gaps in the thick foliage. A man's shout vibrated in the air. Duncan dismounted in a running leap, pulling out his pistol, and bounded over a fallen log toward the sound. Breathing hard, he crouched as he crept toward the tree, frowning as the man's voice babbled in fear, begging to be let go.

What trickery was this?

He rounded a huge oak and pulled up short.

A redcoat deserter, more than a head taller than Miss Rothbury was cowering against the trunk of the tree, begging for his life. On the ground was another redcoat, lying in a pool of blood, his body still and twisted in a way that could only mean death.

All of Duncan's senses, already on high alert, sharpened to the point of pain. His lips pulled back from his teeth, and he sucked in great lungfuls of air as the coppery scent of blood hit his nostrils. He edged around the little clearing trying to see what weapon Frances had.

God's blood, what the hell was going on here? Frowning as he crept forward, he craned his neck.

Without warning, Frances took another step toward the redcoat and swung out with her bloodied hand in a blur of movement.

Duncan leapt forward with a roar. "Frances!"

He brought his gun up. The burly bastard in front of her had a knife—

The deserter lunged, but she was too fast, too strong, evading the thrust of the knife with ease. She grabbed the wrist of the hand holding the knife and squeezed, and the Deserter howled, falling to his knees

"You won't get the children!" she snarled. Whipping through the air in a blur of movement, her clawed hand struck at his throat.

He fell in a spray of blood. It was over in seconds.

Duncan inhaled sharply and by degrees, lowered the gun. He took a few vital moments to try and understand what he'd just seen, blinking to help his dry, painful eyes.

As leaves rustled in the tree overhead, his fingers clenched around the gun again and he looked up, sagging against the trunk when he saw his children. The relief nearly undid him. *They were safe.* And Brodie had his hands over Roslyn's eyes. Aye, the boy was clever.

Duncan put his fingers to his lips.

Brodie nodded despite his white face.

Duncan rounded another tree. Every muscle in his body froze when he caught sight of Frances' face. He knew instantly why the deserter had been desperate to get away.

Her eyes glowed an iridescent blue, her deadly gaze on the man who lay dying on the ground. His lifeblood pumped onto the ground, his throat torn to shreds. Two of her blood-stained fingers still curled in the death blow, her arm outstretched as she watched him like a predator. The useless tendons and muscles in his shredded neck still tried to work and then stopped altogether.

The man was dead. Two dead men. And yet his governess and his children lived.

"*Berserker*," he breathed.

Her cheekbones were sharp, her skin like pale ice, her lips red as blood. And her eyes! The blood in Duncan's veins surged with heat at her ferocious beauty, spreading through his body like molten lava.

Shouts preceded the men from the castle as they crashed through the undergrowth.

"Jesus, Mary and Joseph." Malcolm's voice came first. "Witch!"

He wheeled around, giving his friend a searing look as he pushed Malcolm back toward the edge of the wood. *"Shut up* Malcolm. Not another word. She's no witch."

He saw Malcolm's lips tighten with mutiny, his gaze as sharp as a blade. "I mean it, you'll say no word about it. I'll have your loyalty on this."

A tense moment ensued before Malcolm spat, and muttered, "Aye."

More men followed, but Malcolm stopped them from moving forward at an angle where they could see Miss Rothbury's face.

"Get back," Duncan ordered through clenched teeth. When they didn't move, he roared, "All of you! Get back!"

They moved back toward the edge of the wood as commanded.

Duncan prowled forward very slowly, ensuring that he kept himself within her peripheral vision.

He kept his voice very low. "Miss Rothbury," he said quietly.

That deadly blue gaze did not move off the deserter.

"Miss Rothbury," he said, moving more into her line of vision. "Look at me."

Her face turned toward him, but her eyes did not move.

Duncan tried again. "Miss Rothbury, look at me. It's the Laird."

He called her name at a couple more times, but she would not look at him. Finally, he tried her first name. "Frances, it's Duncan. Look at me."

A frown marred her forehead and for the first time she blinked.

Duncan took a deep breath and shut his eyes for a moment, feeling the sweat trickle between his shoulder blades despite the chill of evening coming down quickly.

"Frances, can you hear me?"

She blinked again.

Using the voice he favoured for training skittish horses, he coaxed her down from the fury until the blaze in her blue eyes started to dim. He watched as she swayed and then looked around carefully, as though rousing from a deep sleep, with the knowledge she would find herself in unfamiliar terrain.

"Frances," he said gently.

Her gaze met his, panic in her expression as her breathing sped up to an alarming rate.

"The children?" she choked, "Are the children—?"

"They're safe. Brodie and Roslyn are safe." He took a step toward her, his hands up as he attempted to soothe her.

She immediately backed away, her agitation increasing, her fingers clenching into fists. Where her skin had been ice pale, colour now flooded into her cheeks.

"Frances, it's all right, stay where you are, they're safe—"

A gasp cut him off as she looked at her trembling, blooded-stained hand, shudders shaking her small frame as she saw the dead men. "Oh, no." She moaned. "Oh, God. No." With frantic eyes her gaze darted around like a dragonfly as she took a step back, and then another, before she turned and ran.

～

*S*he would be sent to the gallows. Her life was over. Not only had she put the Laird's children in danger, she had revealed a secret that she should have taken to her grave.

Frances was fast in her desperation to get away but didn't get far. The Laird moved with a speed that belied his size. Exhausted, she tried to evade him by ducking into a thicket of dense bush, knowing he'd be hampered by his bulk.

That worked for less than a minute.

A strong, warm arm snaked around her waist and hauled her off her feet.

"No!" she screamed. Her voice cracked as she summoned the last of her reserves and twisted, arching her head back to smack him senseless.

She needed to be free to run as far away from the horror she'd created as she could go.

She had to keep everyone safe from the beserker. From her. The children...oh, God, the children had seen her.

"Damn it, Frances!" Duncan ducked his head to the side, his free hand fastened gently around her throat, holding her immobile as he backed out of the thicket.

Frances slumped, shudders shaking her frame as it moulded to his much larger one.

"There now, lassie. There now."

She felt rather than heard his voice, the deep vibration against her neck, the warmth of his breath, the rumble of it soothing against her back. She made a weak attempt at trying to move his arms, her fingers trying to pry them away, but had nothing left.

He was no friend to offer comfort. The last few months had been a sham, a dream she'd used to her reality, like a gay tea cosy that covered the dregs of a cold pot of tea.

Her stomach heaved and she sagged against him, trying to breathe through her nose.

And she had killed. Again.

The feel of her fingers, ripping and tearing through the flesh of that man's neck...

Frances gagged and was immediately bent over so the she could void her stomach. The warmth of his body behind hers should have provided comfort but it did not.

No comfort for a murderess.

She spat as delicately as she could, taking great heaving breaths.

"Let…let me go," she ground out in a hoarse voice.

"Come to the stream to rinse your mouth."

It was not a suggestion. He led the way, a strong arm around her waist, mostly holding her up as she stumbled through the thick foliage until they came to a little clearing and the stream. Bending at the waist, he scooped up a handful of water for her to drink.

She obeyed, taking a mouthful from his cupped hands. But when she went to spit it out, she caught sight of her bloody hands. Whirling, she waded into the stream, uncaring of her shoes and skirts, bending to scrub her skin with feverish intensity.

"Frances."

She ignored him, plunging her hands back into the water, panting with the effort of trying to cleanse the blood.

"Fran. Stop."

When she realised her sleeve was stained with blood, she rose, her cold fingers fumbling with the buttons of her outer coat. She made a frustrated sound when she couldn't get them through the holes fast enough and wrenched the edges apart, buttons plopping into the water.

"Fran."

"Get it off," she cried out, "Get it off me!"

He strode into the stream and with no effort, tore the last three buttons off to free her of the jacket. Immediately she yanked off the arms and threw the jacket into water. Shivering, she wrapped her arms around herself and watched it in the bleak silence as it floated downstream.

How long they stood in the stream, Frances didn't know. She didn't want to break the silence. For when the silence ended, so did her freedom, the peace of the last four months, everything she'd never dared to hope for.

She jerked wildly when something touched her arm and looked down, dismayed to see the Laird's long, blunt fingers on her pale, cold skin.

"Frances."

"I did not give you leave to use my first name." Her voice was harsh in the silence.

"Look at me."

She looked up for a moment and met his gaze until shame forced her eyes down again.

"You're a *beserker*."

Her trembling lips pinched together to hear the word aloud. "I don't wish to discuss it."

He made a derisive sound. "You don't have that option right now."

Angling her chin, she nevertheless kept her gaze averted. "I won't talk about it."

Another shiver shook her frame and the hand on her arm tightened.

"Come out of the stream before you catch your death."

She allowed herself to be led out, grateful for his strength as she slipped on the smooth, pebbled rocks. Once out, however, she pulled her arm back to dislodge his hold but his hand tightened. Why wouldn't he let her be? He was standing so close she could feel the heat wafting off his body.

Despite the shivers and a creeping exhaustion that always followed an episode, Frances rallied.

"I need to leave."

"You're not going anywhere."

Startled, she looked up. The Laird's intent gaze collided with hers and her heart sank. She knew him enough to recognise the determination in his eyes.

"I resign my—"

"Tell me what happened."

Her lips trembled but stayed firmly shut.

"They were going to harm the children?"

She swallowed. "Yes." Talking through the lump in her throat was a mighty effort.

"You protected them. You saved them."

Frances swayed with relief but kept her gaze on the water tumbling over the rocks in the stream. She took in a deep, shuddering breath and then looked at him. "You should be with your children now. I will…I will follow later and pack my—"

He arched a brow and moved closer. "You're not going anywhere."

Frances tried to step back, but he still grasped her arm, his warm hand tightening on her cold skin.

"Remember: I'm Laird on this land. You're staying here until I decide the best course of action."

Frowning, she tried to make sense of his implacable words. "B-but, you…you'll be harbouring a fugitive. I won't stay here and endanger you all. I won't." She shook her head.

Silent, he just watched her, and she saw the moment his gaze travelled lower than her face.

Instantly, heat rose in her cheeks and she shrank back. Or tried to, but her efforts were in vain. "You can't keep me here—"

Frances broke off as his expression changed momentarily, determination and something else, something so acutely male she couldn't even name. Alarmed, she yanked her arm free. "I'm not staying here."

A muscle jumped in his jaw, the hard planes of his face like granite. "Come. You're exhausted, cold and no doubt in need of a brandy and the warmth of the kitchen. We'll go back to the castle—"

"Stop treating me like a child! I will not stay after what has transpired."

His gaze narrowed at her tone.

That was her only warning before he moved with a speed she thought impossible. One moment she was standing at least an arm's length away and the next, she was engulfed in the warm, masculine strength of his arms.

"On the contrary," he ground out between clenched teeth, "I do not think of you like any child."

This time Frances looked at him, looked deep into his eyes and saw what she'd been trying so hard to ignore. He still wanted her, despite all he'd seen. Despite her secret.

He was the Laird, and on his lands, he was ruler supreme.

Frances quailed, some secret, feminine part shrinking from the dominance she sensed in him.

She could not stay!

Swallowing, she fought for control. She could reason in any situation; reason had worked for her in nearly every fraught encounter. This was no different.

Without breaking his gaze, she spoke in a fierce undertone, "Laird Grant, I put your children in danger and *murdered two men*. I must resign my post and leave to ensure the safety of your people, your clan. *You. Your own children*. I cannot stay here."

He watched her with a narrowed gaze.

She waited, trapped in his embrace, his hand clenched in the hair at her nape, holding her immobile, his face scant inches away.

"Your story lacks truth. While on my land, you and my children should never be in danger. Those men were trespassing, and you acted in self-defence. T'was not murder." He shook his head, the hand around her nape lifted to cup her jaw. "Let me help you, Frances."

She almost succumbed to the desire to let him. Her lips trembled, her gaze captured by his, unable to look away as she tried to speak, to break the lure he represented; protection, security and warmth. Oh, why wouldn't her voice work?

At her silence, his gaze narrowed with a deep intensity that made the muscles in her stomach clench. "You're staying here. Where I can protect you."

And when her lips tightened in mutiny, he added, "You'll not leave. That's my direct order."

CHAPTER SIX

*D*uncan returned to ensure his children's wellbeing, all but dragging Frances back with him. Keeping her within his sight, he stalked over to his man. "Fergus. Gather a few men. The bodies will need to be removed, take them as far as you can. Take the little used track."

"Aye, Laird." Fergus frowned down at the bodies and spat. "Deserters. What hap—"

Duncan narrowed his eyes at the man. "Miss Rothbury was teaching archery to the children when she happened to come upon the dead bodies of two deserters. Their throats had been ripped out."

Fergus' expression sharpened. And then he nodded, despite the clear evidence of seeing with his own eyes that one of the men had still been alive when they'd arrived on the scene. "The black dog, you be thinking Laird?"

"Aye, these are dangerous times," Duncan responded, deliberately fostering the ancient tale.

"Then we'll have to send a warning out, to ensure no one else runs a-foul of it."

Duncan inhaled and answered with a hard smile and a nod, "Aye. Far and wide, Fergus."

"Aye, Laird." Fergus turned away and called out for the men he needed.

Turning his attention to the two bodies, Duncan hunkered down, noting their tattered coats, the badges removed. Dispassionate, he looked at their wounds and remembered Frances' deadly expression.

Now he knew her dreams, and her deepest secret. He huffed out a breath. More like her darkest nightmare. Her fierce expression during her dream, the slashing motion; it all clicked into place. Shaking his head, he rose.

Duncan looked at the dead bodies of the men who would have most likely raped and murdered his governess and done the same to his children. His gaze lifted to them, huddled next to Frances, who was draped in a plaid someone had provided.

In his colours.

Something primitive stirred in the pit of his gut.

Something possessive and shocking in its potency. He'd never felt this way before about a woman —*any woman*. Despite her ordeal, her shoulders were straight, her neck unbent.

For a month he'd wondered and agonised at how he would break the impeachable wall she'd put up between them. And now it had all come crashing down. Now, she couldn't ignore him and by God, he was done with waiting for answers.

She had both arms around his children, her fingers curled around their shoulders as they leaned into her. He watched as her tender fingers tucked a stray lock of Roslyn's hair behind her ear and that same tender hand tucked his daughter closer for comfort.

As soon as they'd been plucked from the tree, the children had rushed straight toward their governess. Duncan had watched as Frances held herself away, but Roslyn had flung herself against Frances' side. And Brodie, after hesitating, had done the same.

After a moment, Frances had crumbled, crouching down to gather them both into her arms. The stark expression on her white face was something Duncan would never forget; the intensity of it burning a hole in his heart. There was no doubt she loved his children as her own and it was something he'd shamelessly use in bid to have her by his side.

As his wife.

His decision made, he walked toward them, noting when Frances became aware of his proximity.

She stiffened and stepped back from his children.

His gaze narrowed on hers and his lips curled in a hard smile as she raised her chin, expecting no less.

Hunkering down in front of the children, he gathered them close. "Roslyn and Brodie, you must thank Miss Rothbury for saving your life."

"Aye," Brodie nodded.

"Papa, I was so scared. Brodie covered my eyes and I couldn't see anything. But I kept very quiet, like he told me."

Duncan hugged her, "Aye my special girl, you were very brave." He looked at his son, inclining his head. Brodie nodded, his eyes communicating the answer to the unspoken question. Duncan curled his fist and gently bumped Brodie's heart, then gathered the boy close.

Frances' secret was safe.

He then saw Malcolm, standing apart from the others. Duncan knew what the mutinous expression on Malcolm's face meant. He inhaled then let out a noisy breath and stood. "Stay with Miss Rothbury, children."

Malcolm's eyes narrowed as Duncan approached.

"She's a witch, Duncan. Don't try to convince me otherwise."

"She's not a witch." Duncan placed his hand on Malcolm's shoulder. "She's a *beserker*. Remember that old—"

"Aye, I know the *legend*, Duncan. And even if it were true, no woman could ever be that strong to rip out a man's throat. She's a witch." He shrugged his shoulder to dislodge Duncan's hand.

"Malcolm—"

"Christ man, have you forgotten Marie so quickly?" His friend's expression was fierce. "English women canna survive here. Have you forgotten losing her, the anguish of it for your children? Of not being able to help her? Miss Rothbury is a witch. Or does being the Laird mean you're just like your father, an English-loving *bastard*, thinking with your cock and not for the good of your clan!"

Duncan caught Malcolm's shirt and hauled him close until they were nose to nose. Through gritted teeth, he spoke, "It's because I think of you like a brother that my fist is no' connecting with your face." He inhaled to try and clear the anger beating the air between them.

Duncan's grip tightened when Malcolm tried to free himself, and he bared his teeth.

"I was a dutiful husband to Marie. I did my best to make Marie as comfortable as possible. People die, Malcolm, some before their time. I can't sit in the dark pining forever. It's been *eight years*. And we both know the reason for your anger; it's not Marie, and it's not Miss Rothbury. It's your sister—"

Malcolm's hand came up to clench Duncan's wrist and yanked.

Duncan resisted; his knuckles white. He wasn't finished. "Aye, think about your anger, *brother*. You, who's always protected women. Miss Rothbury might be English, but she saved my children and herself from the very fate your sister couldn't avoid.

Why she's your target against those you've never been able to find and bring to justice, I *dinna ken*. Vengeance burns your soul, Malcolm. Let it go before it burns away your good sense, too."

For a moment they both strained together until Malcolm pushed Duncan away with a disgusted sound. "She's a bloody English witch—"

"She's no' a witch." Duncan stared him down, uncaring of his guttural tone. "And if I hear rumours to that effect, I'll know the source. If your vengeance hasn't burned all your good sense, and your loyalty away, then you owe me this."

Malcolm dropped his gaze, his breath coming fast between his clenched teeth before he looked at his Laird. "You have my loyalty."

"Aye. And you have mine. As you always have."

They both stared at each other before Duncan gave a curt nod and swung on his heel to return to his children.

He could feel his friend's burning gaze on his back and heard the whisper Malcolm thought wouldn't carry on the wind.

"*You* have my loyalty. But not for that English witch."

Other than his fingers curling into a fist, he gave no indication he heard, but his heart sank.

~

The next morning, Frances stood near the castle entry way and grasped a fistful of her skirts with cold fingers. Surrounded by the Laird's men, their expressions sombre but respectful, their implacable direction only gave her one choice—she was to wait for the Laird. They would not answer her questions but all six of them surrounded her, keeping the worst of chill wind at bay.

Was he going to banish her now? He must, given the circumstances. Surely he'd let her pack her belongings?

"Come Miss Rothbury."

Snapped out of her grim musings, she started when the Laird's men picked her up. "What are you do—?" Frances gasped as they lifted her onto the Laird's horse. She'd not even noticed or heard the animal being brought up.

Duncan vaulted up behind her, his warmth immediately sinking through the clothing at her back.

She stiffened as he settled an arm around her waist, tucking her against him.

"Fergus. Keep an extra watch posted."

Fergus, not one for smiling, inclined his head. "Aye Laird. Tis already organised."

As Duncan urged the horse forward, Frances saw Malcolm leaning against the entry, the cold disapproval in his gaze lacerating her already abraded nerves. She tore her gaze away and tried to slither out of the saddle, but the Laird tightened his arm. She was staying put.

"Where are we going?" Exhaustion and anxiety echoed in her shrill question.

"To someplace we can be alone."

Frances couldn't get her sluggish brain to work as the Laird guided Sterrm through the southern field, toward the thick forest she'd often walked in. Last night had been a blur. She'd barely eaten, her stomach in knots from the afternoon's events. Now the threat hanging over her head had solidified into a terrifying tangibility.

Sleep had not come; seemingly every time she dropped off, she jerked awake with the horror slicing into her consciousness like a blade. Breakfast was difficult. Her anxiety, already high, was made even more so with the murmurs of those around her. The questions from those not at the castle the previous evening wanting her side of the story.

The story Duncan had made her repeat over and over again until she didn't have to think about it.

And Malcolm. Cunning he was, waiting until she was so tired and terrified, waiting until Duncan was distracted, to sit next to her, his expression carefully blank as he questioned her like the finest interrogator. His quiet voice asking her how she'd killed those men, the look in his eyes like a murderous blade on his handsome face.

His hatred of her was palpable when she'd refused to answer any of his questions.

Now she was atop the Laird's horse, going who knew where? With a man determined to have his answers. Ones she most emphatically did not want to impart.

The rhythmic canter of the horse made her eyelids droop, but she forced them open, recognising no landmarks, the farthest she'd ever been on the Laird's lands.

She was so *tired.*

Her eyes closed it seemed for a second, only to fly open as her whole body jerked.

"Sshh, *Sassenach,* sleep if you want. I'm here. We've a-ways to go yet."

Duncan's voice seemed to wrap around her, as warm as the plaid he'd covered them both with. She couldn't help but sink against him, her head lolling against his shoulder as they rode through the forest along a path she could barely see…

~

Frances was deliciously warm. Aware of the chill in the air, she wriggled her toes and stretched her feet. Despite the darkness, she knew it was nearly time to rise. The children would be—

The children.

Inhaling sharply, Frances sat up, looking around the unfamiliar room in the dim light of the banked fire. Cold air raised goosebumps and she realised she was only in chemise. Where was she? And why was she only in her chemise? The last thing she remembered was being on a horse.

With the Laird.

Her heart skipped a beat.

"Morning lass."

Her goosebumps grew more goosebumps. *That deep voice.*

Straining to see him in the gloom, she grasped the blankets to her chin and subsided back into the warmth of the bed.

"Laird Grant." She hated her thin voice.

She remembered now, vague snatches of riding for what seemed like a long time. Being taken down from the horse and inside the cottage. The comfort of the bed, of nightmares and being held through them, given water and then blissful sleep without waking.

A dark shape blocked the meagre glow of the fire and she realised he was building it to heat the room. As the light intensified, so did her trepidation. "Where are my clothes?"

"They're here." He pointed at her dress draped over the chair.

"Did you...?"

"Aye, I wanted you comfortable so you could sleep."

Despite his grave tone, Frances wondered which gave out more heat; the rapidly growing fire in the hearth or the blush that lit her cheeks. "You've taken too many liberties."

"Aye."

The deep timbre of his voice was like a caress.

Frances lay there, wondering what she was going to do.

"Come, you've slept most of yesterday and all night. I'll leave you to dress while I see to providing something to eat."

Relieved when he shut the door, she took care of necessities and dressed, knots of tension returning to tighten the muscles in her stomach.

After they'd eaten, she stayed at the table and watched as the sun rose in the morning sky while he tended the fire. She kept her gaze away from the Laird, looking out the window. Overnight, a frost had formed, everything covered in a film of ice. She looked around the warm, simple cottage. "Who owns this place?"

"I do. It's a hunting cottage, used every so often." Duncan had dusted his hands from the wood and ash and was now sat on a rough stool near the fire, whittling, his back half to her. She could see the masculine jut of his jaw, roughened with new beard. As he whittled, she watched the play of muscles in his shoulders with the rhythmic movement.

Grinding her teeth, she said the words she most emphatically did not want to say. "Laird Grant, why are we here?"

For a moment, only the sound of the small knife shaving through the wood answered her. "Here, I'm not the Laird."

She frowned, but before she could ask what he meant, he continued, "And you're not a governess. This place here, it's our safe place."

His meaning became instantly clear. Her heart jumped and she swallowed at the implication of such intimacy.

"Laird Gra—"

"Duncan, lass."

"I need to go back to the castle. The children—"

"Are fine." He turned, just enough so she could see his profile. "I want the story, Frances. All of it, starting from when you were a bairn."

No one had ever wanted her story. Leaning her elbow on the table, she rubbed her forehead and inhaled deeply. When her brother had died, her story had been locked within her. Not another living soul knew.

Closing her eyes, she wondered when the secret she'd shouldered for so long had become so heavy to bear. The temptation to unburden was so great, she had to bite the inside of her cheek to prevent the words from spilling out.

Could she?

Frances remained silent as she grappled with the habit of a lifetime. He'd seen her as full *beserker*, had seen what she'd done, the monster she became. He'd risked his life to talk her down from the cursed possession.

And now he'd bought her to this place. And they were alone. Audibly exhaling, she straightened, placing her hands in her lap, trying to still her trembling lips.

He'd seen her...

"I..It is inherited. My...my mother never suffered the affliction." She kept her eyes on the tartan fabric covering her lap, couldn't bear to look at him as her fingers worried the hem of his plaid. "She was horrified when she found out. My grandmother suffered it, you see. It skipped a generation."

The whittling continued. "Did you ever meet your grandmother?"

"No. My mother was estranged from her family. I never met any of them."

"And what of your father, lass? What did he think?"

"He never knew. My mother made sure of that. He was not a demonstrative man; my brother and I were kept out of his way most of the time."

"So your father never saw when the change came upon you?"

"No."

"How?"

"My mother instructed me. I was never to lose my temper or place myself in situations where I could lose control. I was to compose myself at all times."

"Do they still live?"

"No." Quiet for a moment, she remembered that awful time, blotting tiny beads of sweat from her lip. "My parents died in a carriage accident when I was eleven."

The whittling stopped for a small moment. "I'm sorry for your loss, Fran. What happened to you after that?"

"My father's solicitor told us that our father had left no will and a distant cousin laid claim to our family's estate. We had to leave."

Frances stopped, her eyes closing as the memories she'd tamped down came rushing at her.

"What happened, lass, tell me all of it." Duncan didn't look at her, but his tone demanded answers. "Where did you go?"

She blinked back her tears. "We had no money, nothing but the few clothes we could pack into a bag. My brother, John refused to let me work. He took his responsibility very seriously. He tried so hard, but he was too old to apprentice and too young for experience. He finally found a good employer, but within the year he..." Frances tried to clear her throat, her voice hoarse, "...He died of scarlet fever."

The whittling stopped. "Ah, lass. You were alone in the world."

"Yes," she whispered, her voice thick with unshed tears at his understanding of her plight.

"But you survived."

"Yes."

"How, Frances? An outbreak of scarlet fever is dangerous."

"I…I don't get sick. I've never been sick."

"You became a governess?" He continued to whittle, and the comforting sound somehow gave her the courage to continue.

"It took a while. I started as a lady's maid. Because of my education, I managed to find work in a governess agency three years ago. I have been blessed." She closed her eyes again. "So many things could be worse."

"And it was something worse that happened to make you flee to Scotland?"

Frances didn't answer, shame and fear rising in equal measure. Her hand stole around her middle as she battled the nausea that rose with them.

"Tell me lass. I know you wouldn't have come to Scotland otherwise."

She watched him, studying his profile. His strong, familiar features bought comfort. Here, she was safe. She could do this. She could tell him. "I was sent to Ashburn Manor for a position with Lord Ashburn. I quickly learned never to be caught alone with him. But one night, he…" Frances trailed off, dabbing at the cold sweat that sprang on her upper lip.

"Go on, lass."

Scrunching her eyes shut, she continued, "He came to my room, quite late. I woke to him holding his hand over my mouth. He was trying to rip open my night rail. I-I tried to scream but his whole weight was on me, his hand on my mouth. It was all I could do to breathe."

"He raped you."

Duncan's deep voice was flat, but she heard the rage beneath it.

"N-no."

The silence was absolute, and she desperately wanted to hear the sound of his whittling. Instead, he turned to face her, and she felt her fingers curl into fists, her nails digging into her palms.

"Go on, Fran."

"He…tried but once my wits woke up, the…m-monster…" She choked on the word. "…It took over. I killed him. When I came to…to myself, I had already fled into the night."

"What did he do to you, Fran?"

She shook her head. She couldn't, it was so embarrassing, so awful.

In a gentle voice, he bade, "Tell me, sweetling. Did he touch you between your legs? Nod if you can't say the words."

She swallowed and nodded with jerky movements of her head.

"With his fingers?"

She nodded again, feeling the heat creep into her cheeks.

"He hurt you." The anger in Duncan's voice gave her hope.

"Yes."

"How did you end up here?"

"My agency. It's run by women." Frances uncurled her aching fingers and squeezed her hands together. "They had your father's request for a governess, so I was sent immediately, the next day."

The tension escalated in the ensuing silence. The more it lengthened, the more agitated Frances became until she broke and lunged for the door, her face hot with humiliation. What must he think of her? *She shouldn't have told him!*

She should have learned from her attempt to escape the day before. He was too quick; his reflexes faster than they should have been for a large man. He caught her round the waist with both arms, turning her so they were face to face.

"Let me go!"

She fought against him until she tired, her fists against his chest. Breathing harshly, she ground out, "You have to let me go."

"Haven't you noticed yet, Frances?"

"Noticed what?" She tried to hold herself away from him, her muscles tense. He simply held her, tightening his arms so she lay against his body, tucking her head against his shoulder as though she were a child.

"I'm not scared of you."

Frances couldn't think of anything to say. Dumbfounded, she tried to understand what he meant.

"Aye, lass," he said with quiet emphasis. "I'm not scared of your *beserker*."

Had he listened to anything she'd said? "I could kill you! Or anyone when I'm angry. From one heartbeat to the next. You *must* understand—"

A warm hand cupped her nape and pulled her head back. "Nay. Understand this, sweetling: I'm not scared of you."

Frances looked at him, searching his grey eyes. What did he mean? All she saw was an implacable warmth…as though…he *cared* for her.

"It comes out to protect you and others in times of danger, doesn't it? That is all, only when there's danger."

"I can't…" She shook her head. Her lips trembled, as did the tears filling her eyes, threatening to fall.

"Ssh, lass, it's alright." He drew her head back to his shoulder again and tenderly kissed her forehead.

She managed to swallow around the lump in her throat, and with a sudden whirl, tore herself out of his arms, moving across the other side of the room. "Why aren't you listening to me? I'm a monster! A beast!" Her chest rose and fell in time with her erratic breathing.

"Nay, Frances, you're not a beast. Let me prove it to you."

"You don't know, so how can you say that? I'm a nightmare," she whispered the last in harsh tones, her hands coming up to cover her face as she gave the horror a voice. "I can't control it."

"That's a matter of opinion."

She lowered her hands.

His expression morphed into a determination that scared her. "You've controlled it plenty since you've come to my castle."

She vented a mocking laugh. "You have no idea. I nearly…" She stopped and then inhaled through her teeth, wanting, *needing* to make him understand. "I nearly killed you the night Brodie was burned."

The air between them vibrated with tension.

He watched her carefully. "The *beserker* came out? Why?"

In harsh tones, she almost spat at him, "Because. I thought you were harming him when I heard him screaming. It was only when I saw the flames on the shirt you ripped off him that I understood."

Breathing in agitated gasps, she felt the ice rise.

Duncan started to walk toward her.

She took a step back. "Stay away from me."

"You're not a monster, Frances. Aye, lass, I'll say it again." He nodded as he advanced. "I'm not scared of you."

She took another step back, her eyes wide.

"I'm not worried about my children with you."

Another step, and her back hit the wall.

"I'm not worried about my clan with you."

She tried again. "How can you be so sure? What right do you have to make that decision? If one of them threatened me, if I thought I was going to be harmed I would kill them." She pointed her finger at him. "What Laird would deliberately endanger his clan in this way?"

A muscle jumped in his jaw and he stopped as he narrowed his gaze. "All my clan see is a woman who extends her heart, who is kind and fair and learned. They love the way you keep the children occupied, how you treat everyone with respect, how you go out of your way to help them. They know, as do I, that you would never think to harm them. They love you…as do I."

Her lips trembled. Everything she'd never dared to hope for was standing in front of her.

But she could never have it.

"What about Malcolm? He is your man, your closest friend. He doesn't hide his hatred of me."

"You've naught to worry about in Malcolm. The man has his own demons. Stop trying to bait me, Frances. It won't work."

Frances sneered. "That's right, how could I forget, you men have the luxury of venting your anger whenever you want! God forbid a woman would have the brain to say what is needed and have *a man* bloody listen." She gritted it out between clenched teeth.

His gaze narrowed and he took a step towards her. "I'll listen when you've got something to say worth listening to. And women get angry. You only have to hear the shouts and pots and pans clanging in the kitchen to stay well away from Mrs Cullen."

Her eyes narrowed into slits as she hissed at him,

"You'd know nothing about having to subdue your anger until you're *choking on it*."

His two hands slapped the wall either side of her head and she inhaled sharply.

"I know what it is to be subdued. To be helpless." He voice deepened as he ground out the words. "My father shipped me from here to London, to boarding school. He wanted me to be more *English*. You would know what it is to be separated from you kin, your home. To have *nothing* of comfort."

As a muscle jumped in his jaw and his grey gaze bored into hers, all she could do was draw in shallow breaths.

"Aye, the pain and loss and bewilderment. The unforgiving bastards who watched me struggle to survive the beatings from the teachers and peers simply because of my accent and my heritage. Do not tell me I lack *understanding*."

She swallowed, watching with wary eyes, her heart feeling sore and old.

His hand came up to cup her jaw, and the harshness in his voice softened. "I *know*, Frances—"

She put her fingers against his mouth to stop his words, grappling with shame as she choked out, "You *don't know*! You know nothing of having this…this power, this monster inside you. Inside *me*. Women are expected to endure, to be demure. Anger is not option for us. For me. *Especially for me*."

His fingers wrapped around hers and he kissed them, watching her with a frown. "Say what you mean."

Her lips trembled. She shook her head.

"Explain, Frances."

For a moment, there was silence except for the sway of trees in the wind, some of their limbs brushing the sides of the cottage.

"You men. You…" She drew in a frustrated breath,

"You fight…from early on violence is…it's *acceptable*.
My mother shunned me, taught me to smother my
anger, to just accept, never question, show no emotion. When you're a girl, there is no expectation of
violence. We are not equipped to deal with it."

She pushed away from him, pressing a shaking
hand to her head. "I can't…I can't explain any more.
You must understand I cannot control it."

Frances heard him exhale. Warm, gentle hands
grasped her arms and turned her back. She looked up
to see him frown, then he looked away and she could
see him, pondering her words.

When his gaze came back to her, his look was focused and intent. "What did you feel, when you saw
those men?"

Frances wet her lips and slid her gaze away from
his. "I was scared."

He shook his head. "No. When you knew they
were going to harm the children?"

A muscle jumped in her jaw, and she shook her
head.

"Say it, Frances."

Mutinous, she pressed her lips together.

"It's like poison if you lock it inside you. Say it!"
he demanded.

She grated the words out through clenched teeth.
"I wanted to kill them!"

He nodded. "Aye, and so you should. I would, too.
Worthless bastards, to prey on women and children."

She felt her eyes crease into slits, her breath
coming rapidly between her lips. "I would do so
again if someone came near your children. *You can't
stop me.*"

A reckless, approving grin stretched his lips. "Aye,
I can't stop you. And I would 'na."

Her brows drew together, the rage she could feel
seeping into her blood waning. "What?" she breathed.

He rubbed her arms. "Even If I could, I wouldn't stop you, not for bastards like that."

Understanding softened his gaze. "I know what you're about. You're not some indiscriminate murderer, Frances. This whole time, your eyes have been glowing like a hot flame, and you haven't killed me. I'm not scared of you."

He bent then, and kissed her, his lips soft and gentle. "I love *all* of you, as you are. Even your anger and your power. It's a part of *you*."

The tears overflowed and poured down her cheeks.

Duncan made a thick sound in his throat and kissed her damp eyes.

She tried to stem her sobs, but they wouldn't stop. He took her in his arms, holding her against his warm, strong body and sat down on one of the large armchairs next to the bed, tucking her onto his lap. "Ah, lass. Your tears fair wrench my heart. Have you been carrying around this burden your whole life? How long has it been since you've had someone to offer comfort?"

Never. Her mother had shunned touching her. Her father had never hugged her. Once her brother knew, he'd become fearful of her, barely speaking to her and jerking back if she came too close to him.

The comfort Duncan provided...it was like nothing she'd ever experienced.

He held her, rubbing her back until her tears stopped. She inhaled deeply to let out a big, shuddering sigh, somehow feeling tired despite her long sleep, and more relaxed than she'd ever felt in her life. She cuddled in his arms, her face pressed into the humid warmth of his neck, loathe to leave the security of his embrace. He was the first person who hadn't backed away from her in horror after finding out her secret.

She was never likely to have it again, so she was going savour every last moment. Sadness filled her then. For she still had to leave. Lord Ashburn's men would find her, of that she was certain. *That meant leaving him, and the children.*

"Better?"

He tipped her face up and she nodded. "Yes. Thank you, Laird."

She saw his gaze narrow a fraction. "Duncan, lass," he said with a soft tenderness, softly wiping her tears from the fragile skin beneath her eyes.

CHAPTER SEVEN

As Frances looked deep into his eyes, she saw it all; concern, compassion and deeper, the desire he usually kept restrained but not quite hidden. His lips so close, she remembered the night he'd kissed her, and grappled with a sudden surge of desire, so potent, without even being aware of it, her hand was around the strong nape of his neck, her fingers entwined in his hair, urging his lips to hers.

He stopped, and hovered. "You're sure?"

She'd never been surer in her life and wondered at his ability to hold back, given the want in his gaze. "Oh, yes." And pressed her lips to his.

He stilled, letting her learn the contours of his lips, until she made a tiny sound of frustration and opened her mouth under his. He complied at once, and she revelled in the taste of him as she took the initiative, making a tender, tentative foray with her tongue.

He met her with a caressing lick before withdrawing for more chaste kisses. Before long, she grew maddened with his teasing, and her tongue surged inside with bold, liquid strokes until his tongue twined with hers the way she needed.

Her blood surged like the tide.

Ever so slowly, he withdrew until his mouth hovered above hers and she strained to reach it. His warm breath flowed down the side of her cheek and her neck, and she shivered. Licking her swollen lips, she tried to urge his head down again.

He gave a soft laugh. "There are other places to kiss, lass."

Frowning, Frances sat a little straighter on his lap, unsure of his meaning.

He leaned back against the chair, exposing his neck.

She inhaled, a deep, greedy breath into her suddenly oxygen-deprived lungs.

He hadn't bothered with a jacket, the warmth of the cottage enough to go without. The top button of his shirt was open. Her gaze roamed the strong, smooth column of his neck up to where his morning beard shadowed beneath his jaw. *Good Lord, he was magnificent.*

Her gaze traced back down the flow of muscle and bone to his broad shoulders, and she swallowed to ease her dry throat.

His utter stillness eased some of her wariness and when she looked into his eyes, the approving heat in his gaze made her blush. Before she lost her nerve, Frances leaned forward to kiss where his scent was strongest, male and warm.

She opened her mouth slightly and the taste of him exploded on her tongue. *Salt and man.* The muscles in his neck tightened beneath her mouth. Drawing back, she licked her lips and saw the way his eyes latched onto her mouth, following the movement of her tongue. A muscle jumped in Duncan's jaw but he stayed entirely still, not touching any part of her with his hands.

Bolder now, her lips traced the tendon in his neck

to beneath his ear and then, obeying some unknown instinct, she bit him gently.

Every muscle in his body clenched and he drew in an audible breath.

She scrambled back.

Hard hands stopped her. "Nay lass, there's nothing I'd rather be doing right now than feeling your mouth on me." His voice was impossibly deep and after a moment, he relaxed back into his original position, his hands once again resting on the arms of the chair. "Unbutton my shirt if you want."

For a moment, she watched him with a wary gaze and then she tightened her lips in resolve. Lifting both her hands, her fingers gingerly slipped the buttons from their moorings. Drawing the edges apart, she inadvertently scored the skin of his chest with her nails.

He sucked an audible breath through his teeth and shivered. Fascinated, she watched the nubs of his nipples harden and her own tingled and tightened in a delicious constriction.

It was true—he did like her hands on him.

She did it again, dragging her nails lightly against the muscles of his chest and abdomen. This time he thrust upward with his hips, the hard bulge beneath nudging her bottom. His light grey eyes glowed with desire, his lids at half-mast. A muscle jumped again in his jaw, but he made no move to touch her.

The realisation hit her. His restraint was deliberate, allowing her to set the pace. A warm bubble of emotion rose until it engulfed her heart. It was this knowledge that gave her the courage to straddle his lap. And as she settled, it was her turn to gasp as her sensitive core, already swollen and damp, pressed directly against his erection.

She paused to absorb the sensations and tried to tamp down her instinctive fear of what had happened before. She wet her trembling lips and said, "I-I want to touch you."

The muscles in his throat worked as he swallowed. "You can touch me anywhere you want, sweetling."

She let out a careful breath. "Even…*there?*"

He nodded, the barest sheen of sweat glistening on his brow. She rose on her knees and dragged at handfuls of his kilt. Eyes closed, she reached down and with careful, tentative fingers, explored beneath.

"Hot," she whispered, her breath shallow, scarcely understanding what she said. His shaft was hard, yet the skin was soft as silk. She grasped him in one hand, learning his shape until he was thrusting against her, his head thrown back, his eyes closed, his hands grasping the arm of the chair until his knuckles showed white.

He was breathtakingly beautiful, all hard muscle and bone. She could feel herself melting, the damp heat between her legs growing as she looked down at the sight of her hand around him. Now she understood; the empty ache demanded fulfilment. *She wanted him.*

He grasped her wrist to stay her hand. "Frances, I'm too close…"

Her gaze flew to his in protest. "No, I want to!"

"I don't want to shock you," he said gently, the breath hissing between his teeth as she measured his length again. Before he could speak, she let go and rose on her knees, gathering handfuls of skirt, baring her dark stockings.

His hands on her arms stopped her. "Nay, Frances," he said in a rough growl, "You're not near enough ready."

She shrugged his hands off and continued gathering the fabric until her skirts were out of the way and inched forward.

"You're going to—" he hissed, drawing the air in between his teeth as the damp curls of her sex brushed his cock. He grasped her arms, and spoke through gritted teeth, "I don't…I can't hurt you. I'd rather be…Frances," he ground out in a hoarse voice as she began to sink down on him.

"Ssh," she whispered. "This is *my* choice. You've given me this."

Frances whimpered as she pushed down again; the hot stretch of tissue was immediate and almost unbearable. She rose and tried again, making a pained, frustrated sound as she tried to slide down on him.

When she felt a fleeting stroke against the top of her sex, she gasped.

It flared all the nerves deep in her pelvis with a surprising lash of pleasure.

He repeated the caress.

She sank down a little more, the pleasure and pain combining in repeated caresses until she engulfed him whole. Swallowing, she inhaled as she tried to accustom herself to his girth, blinking the sudden tears from her eyes.

"Lass," he whispered, and cupped her cheek, a tender thumb wiping away the moisture.

The mechanics of sex were not a mystery. Growing up as she'd done, she'd once come upon two servants in the house, hastily coupling in the lee of a stairwell. At first, she'd not understood but then realised what they'd been doing. As she became older there was the talk of a multitude of ladies.

What she'd not understood was the earth-shattering intimacy of it, that the closeness of two people joining could give someone like her the unfamiliar sense of belonging. Just for this once, she would take what she could.

"Are you alright?" Duncan asked, his voice low with tenderness.

She fought her tears. In a moment of blinding clarity, it struck her just how deeply in love she was with him and her lashes swept down lest any of it showed in her eyes.

He was not for her, for she couldn't stay. If the Lord's men caught up with her, she couldn't be here. She would not endanger his clan and his children.

"Yes, I am alright." She whispered her reply.

Another caress surprised a gasp from her, and her muscles tightened around him, as did her hands around his forearms.

"You feel like heaven."

She glanced up to find him watching her.

He held her gaze and caressed her again.

She captured the deep sound of want in her throat.

A smile stretched his lips, stark and wicked as he delicately swirled his thumb against her.

"Can you move, Fran. Or are you still sore?"

Nodding uncertainly, she flexed the long muscles in her thighs and slowly lifted herself, then sank down, hissing at the sting. But he kept stroking her and that far outweighed the discomfort. She wanted more, because what he was doing was driving her mad, building by slow degrees.

Her pleasure rose at every touch of those clever fingers between her legs and each stroke of him inside, until she was panting, the breath rushing from her lungs, driven by an urge she didn't need to understand. Sweat misted her skin as the voluptuous heat became unbearable. She shook her head as the sensation between her legs began to soar. Afraid of losing control, she stopped abruptly.

"No," she whispered on a soft sob. Bad things happened when she lost control. What if the *beserker* rose. What if she couldn't stop it? What if she hurt him?

"Trust me, Fran. We're doing this together." Her eyelids gradually rose, seeing his glittering gaze boring into hers. He moved his hand to entwine his fingers with hers. "Together, lass. I've got you. Don't be afraid."

"Wh-What if I hurt you?"

"We're together."

She swallowed, tears pricking her eyes at the absolute trust in his gaze. And the love. For her. She nodded, rising once more to move with his fingers.

"I bet you're even more beautiful beneath your clothes. I'd like to find out if your breasts are sensitive. I think they are."

Her breathing slowed as she heard the caress in his deep voice.

He'd raised his head, keeping his fingers on her, his mouth close to her ear, the occasional brush of his lips against the delicate outer shell heightening her senses.

"If I could, I'd bare you naked and stoke your breasts until your nipples were like ripe berries. Then I'd lick them, Frances, softly, until you begged me to take them in my mouth. But I'd tease you just a little more."

The heat in her blood quickly became like lava, and his wicked words made it hotter.

"Then I'd suckle them, maybe stroking you like I'm doing now. Would you like that Frances? My mouth on your breasts while I pleasure you between your legs?"

Her head felt too heavy to hold up and she bent forward until her forehead met his, the breath hissing between her teeth, little cries of pleasure saturating the air as she moved faster. The molten sensation between her legs was so strong that she started to slow, scared at the intensity of it, shying away from what the culmination might bring.

"I'm imagining you naked, with your legs spread, the air caressing every inch of your skin as I suckle your nipples—no don't stop, sweetling, don't stop," he growled.

"I-I can't, it's too…much," she gasped.

For the first time, he moved, slinging a muscled arm around her hips and pulling her down, pushing himself deeper than he'd ever been. She whimpered and bucked against him as the first bolt of sensation struck, far beyond any attempt at control.

He did it again and again, until on the third hard stroke she imploded, crying out, blind to anything but the pleasure saturating her entire being.

"Frances," Duncan groaned, as he continued to move within her.

She opened her eyes as he flung his head back, the muscles in his strong neck taut. A flooding warmth filled her, so perfect that she tightened her thighs to hold onto him for as long as she could, wishing she could stay like this with him forever.

~

Frances woke with a start, blinking in the dim light. The candle had almost burned down, barely penetrating the thick darkness. The hand around her breast squeezed gently, testing the resilience of her flesh. She knew immediately who provided the heat at her back and the pleasure already spreading through her blood.

"L-Laird?" Her voice was rough with sleep and desire.

He chuckled softly, "Duncan, lass. How long is it going to take for you to say my name?"

She didn't answer, distracted by the warm hand

around her breast. Her bare breast. And she'd discovered he'd been right. She *was* sensitive; her nipple throbbed as he delicately squeezed it between slightly rough fingers and the sensation shot down to the already damp flesh between her legs.

"Frances? Tell me now if you don't want this and I'll stop."

She nodded, taking shallow breaths and then realised it might be too dark. "Y-yes," she stammered.

Inhaling audibly, she pushed back against him, instinctively trying to increase the contact of their bodies. And froze when she felt his cock against the small of her back.

He pushed against her, a small rough growl against her ear. He was naked.

She let out the breath she'd been holding as he urged her to lie on her back. She still had on her chemise but little good it did, sagging to allow his large, warm hands free reign. And in moments, he'd removed it anyway.

He moved again, his knee intruding between hers, his heat enveloping her side as their bodies touched.

She gasped, loving the sensation of his skin on hers.

The back of his hand came up and stroked her cheek. "You'll be sore still, but I'll go slow and gentle?"

"Yes," she whispered, blushing, some of the tension leaving her muscles. In these matters, she knew nothing, but she completely trusted him.

"Aye, relax *sassenach*. Let me pleasure you this time."

Pleasure her this time? Any more pleasure than the last time and she'd most likely expire!

He kissed her, but not like the last time. He took the lead with slow, deep kisses that had her wrapping her arm around his neck to bring him as close as she could. And when he released her mouth, Frances inhaled deeply, almost gasping for air.

His mouth travelled beneath her jaw.

She arched her neck, shivering as he bit her with delicate precision. She remembered doing the same to him, and now knew how it felt.

He skimmed down her body, shifting lower, his mouth kissing across her collarbone and then down to the upper slope of her breast. Inexplicably, he slowed, kissing the swell of her breast, circling the nipple and nibbling his way down to the sensitive slope beneath.

With gentle teeth, he bit and then licked the tiny sting. Her nipples tightened and she couldn't help but arch her back with a small sound. He did it again and again, kissing his way between the valley of her breasts until she whimpered. "Please, *oh, please.*"

Finally, he took one taut nipple into his mouth and suckled, gently. Too soft.

"Please," she begged, the back of her hand going to her mouth, the other hand shamelessly wrapping around his nape, urging him on. Frances was equal parts mortified and begging. She needed more…

He released her nipple from the hot cavern of his mouth and started again with the leisurely kisses and tingling bites that drove her mad. She could hear panting and realised the rush of inhalation and exhalation was from her.

"I knew you'd be sensitive. Remember what I told you?" He purred against her skin. He wasn't kissing her and she felt the touch of his fingertips skate down her belly, causing a violent shiver that echoed in her sudden, trembling inhalation. He'd shifted during his intimate exploration of her breasts, drawing one knee up and hooking one of her legs over his hip.

She was open for him to explore as he wished.

And in an instant, the wicked, incendiary words he'd whispered in her ear came back…

"…*My mouth on your breasts while I pleasure you between your legs?*"

His fingers wasted no time, delving gently into her wet warmth, discovering the liquid essence of her desire. Frances lay, the back of her hand still against her mouth as her face grew hot.

His fingertip found the source of her pleasure, using her moisture to delicately circle the small knot of flesh with devastating thoroughness.

Her teeth clenched together as the pleasure spread. When his finger penetrated her opening, it didn't hurt. Especially when his thumb resumed the gentle rubbing.

And then his mouth clamped down on her nipple and suckled with the pressure she'd been begging for.

Frances was blind to everything but the desire coursing through her blood, the rhythmic ebb and flow of sensation. She wanted it never to stop.

~

*R*eleasing her nipple, Duncan blew on it and she arched beneath him.

"Look at me, Frances."

Her face turned to him, but her eyes remained closed. He knew she was close; he could feel the sheath surrounding his finger tighten exquisitely.

"Frances, look at me." He needed to see her eyes.

She opened her eyes as he shifted to push another finger in, stretching her, adjusting the angle to put pressure on where she was most sensitive and rubbed her small knot of female pleasure with his thumb.

Her normally soft blue eyes glowed as she climaxed.

Her passionate cry in dim light of the cold, early morning brought him just as much satisfaction as if he'd climaxed with her. He rode her through it, wringing every last drop until she was limp and sated.

Duncan moved over her, wrapping a hand around her wrist and drawing it up over her head. Adjusting himself, he positioned his cock and slowly pushed in, careful of her newly-tried state.

He watched her face, ensuring her comfort until he was all the way in and then stopped so she could adjust to him.

"Alright, lass?" Even he could hear the growl in his voice.

"Yes." It was said on a sigh

Duncan smiled, but knew it held a tinge of desperation. Now that he was inside her, the urge to ride her hard was strong. But the thought of hurting her made him wait, despite the sweat misting his brow and the ache in his loins.

Frances wriggled her pelvis, wrenching a groan from him. It was the signal to move.

He withdrew slowly, feeling every inch of her tight, hot sheath.

She tried to pull her arm down, but he held it fast. Increasing his rhythm until it became sure and steady, pushing all the way in and then dragging his cock slowly out.

Duncan inhaled deeply. He'd never felt this sense of…rightness, of being so in tune with another person. It was like he'd found something he'd never known was missing, like they were halves of a whole.

Her lips parted as she sucked in more air, her thighs pulling further back as she tried to push her pelvis against his. He adjusted his position, tucking his free hand beneath her nape, grasping the soft hair.

"Please, please Laird," she begged.

He covered her mouth, imitating the carnal stimulation with deep, drugging thrusts of his tongue.

Frances arched her pelvis again, trying to make him move faster but he resisted her attempts, keeping the same, steady rhythm. He would not be hurried, he wanted to savour every moment she held him close.

Pulling his mouth away, he thrust again and again, each time losing a little restraint, just a little harder each time. "Frances, say my name," he whispered.

She didn't answer.

He slowed until she cried out, the nails of her free hand scoring the skin on his back.

"Say my name, Frances. Who's inside you?"

"You," she returned.

"Aye, and who am I?"

She remained silent and he slowed further still until she arched. "Please, please."

"Say it," he growled.

"Duncan." The breathy whisper goaded him.

Duncan thrust against her, hard, and felt the muscles in her belly flutter against his.

"Tell me again."

"Duncan," she groaned, her neck arched back as he hooked an arm beneath her knee to cant her pelvis up.

"Duncan," she cried out as he began thrusting faster and harder, his mouth sealing hers until she tore it away, crying out his name again.

He lunged deep, and growled "Let it come, Frances."

And then he gently bit the tendon on the side of her neck.

She convulsed and screamed, squeezing his cock in a flurry of undulations.

He groaned out his pleasure, then hissed against

the humid warmth of her neck as he emptied his seed within her, holding her sealed against him.

His heart soared.

The rightness of their joining cemented what had been fragmented thoughts. Frances was his, and the only way forward from now was nothing less than marriage.

He was never letting her go.

*L*eaning against the wall, Frances watched as Duncan saddled Sterrm. His long fingers were deft and sure as he tightened the cinch for the saddle. She closed her eyes when his deep voice soothed the big beast, remembering the same deep voice murmuring against her ear as he filled her so completely, so utterly deep.

Their time had come to an end.

So had hers.

"Are you dreaming standing up, lass?" Warm arms came around her, holding her close.

"These last two days have been a dream I've wished never to wake from." She whispered against his neck, not able to help caressing his skin with her lips.

He nodded, "Aye. I'm loathe to go back, but we can't stay longer. Not right now."

Drawing in a breath, she nodded too, and stepped back, her heart aching when his arms fell away.

"Of course. I would not expect it of you." She smiled to hide her misery. For when they returned to the castle, she would be preparing to leave.

"What is amiss, Fran?"

"Nothing at all. It's been so…so wonderful."

He watched her carefully, and prepared, she let nothing of her inner emotion to show.

"There's something I want to ask before we return."

Frances tensed. "Oh?"

He searched her expression, before, without warning, he dropped to one knee and took her hand.

For a moment, she didn't understand. And then her eyes widened.

"I have no betrothal ring with me but that does not matter. Frances Rothbury, will you marry me?"

Overwhelmed by a joy so intense, her heart jumped fair out of her chest. And then that bittersweet, familiar reality where things like marriage were not for her crept back in, and her joyful heart had settled into its familiar, lonely rhythm.

"Laird Grant. I…you…" she stumbled, and, gritting her teeth, collected herself for coherency. Tugging on his hand, she pulled until he stood and then let go.

"I cannot marry you."

"Why?"

Her gaze flicked to his and she swallowed, recognising that determined look. She too, had her own determination.

"I am a danger to you clan—"

"I thought we'd been through this well-worn argument?"

"You haven't listened, Laird—"

"And when did it revert to Laird, instead of Duncan?" His narrowed, blistering gaze captured hers. "Or do you only called me 'Duncan' when I'm hilt-deep inside you, feeling you ripple around me like the hottest, softest glove?"

She ground her teeth as heat swept into her cheeks, and the muscles deep in her pelvis clenched in remembrance. *Damn him!* In a voice that shook with anger, she spoke through clenched teeth. "At any given moment, Lord Ashburn's men can ride up to your castle and demand justice." She inhaled and then snarled, "I will *not* have you and your people exposed to the ramifications of my actions any longer. I've already been here too long."

For a moment, they stood glaring at each other like adversaries.

"Fran, stop and think—"

"No! You saw…you saw what I'm capable of. You know that if a band of redcoats came with the Lord's men, your people would be in danger. You and the children would be in danger! I can't have that on my conscience!"

She turned away, her knuckles pressed against her lips as a sob escaped her throat. "I won't have any more death on my conscience."

His warm hand on the crook of her arm stopped her and he drew her into his embrace. She stood stiff and unyielding in his embrace. But after a moment of his warmth, she couldn't help but sink against him.

His hand closed about her nape as his kissed her forehead. "I'll not let any red-coated bastard or Lord's men take you. I can protect you, Frances. Can't you understand?"

For a moment, she wavered, imagining what life would be like if she said yes. To live unguarded, no constant worrying, no anxiety, safe and secure, being loved.

He lifted her chin with a gentle hand and searched her gaze. "I love you. Stop running when there is no need. *Marry me.*"

She loved him so much. So much it hurt…

Lifting her chin away, she looked past his arm and closed herself off. "I'm sorry, Laird Grant. I must refuse your generous offer."

"Frances," he growled.

Lifting her eyes to him, she said the words that

cut deep into her heart. "I-I don't love you. And I'm leaving when we return to the castle."

He said nothing, the tension encasing them rising like a living entity.

When he spoke, his light tone didn't fool her in the slightest. "You don't love me?"

"No."

"You've never taken a man to your bed before."

She felt her cheeks heat instantly. "Laird Grant—"

"I know you haven't."

"What relevance—"

"If you'd been more experienced, you'd know what we shared these last two days was not just sex. Our connection goes beyond anything I've felt before."

"I don't love you."

The side of his mouth quirked and she lifted her chin as the determination in his gaze increased exponentially. She knew that look.

He took the step to close the distance between them and again, his hand came up around her nape. Frances stiffened and tried to step back as he crowded her. His arm went around her.

"Lair—"

His head swooped and she gasped. Just when she thought his lips would cover hers, he stopped. Hovering over her mouth, his lips barely brushed hers.

"I love you, Frances."

She raised herself on tippy-toes, but he teased her, withholding his kiss.

"Marry me."

His lips brushed hers and she tried to follow him, making a sound in her throat when he drew back to hover again.

"Marry me," he said, his voice impossibly deep.

"No."

"Stubborn wench," he growled and kissed her.

Plunged into immediate desire, Frances succumbed without a whimper. His deep, voluptuous kiss was like the ones he'd given her right before he hooked an arm beneath her knee and slowly slid inside her, thrusting until she was clawing his skin to have him go deeper, a little harder…

When he pulled his mouth away, it was a shock to come back to reality. Standing in front of the lean to, where Sterrm patiently waited. Her breath misted the space between them as she mindlessly sought his mouth again.

But he held her fast and shook his head. "Nay, *Sassenach*. You'll not get any more of this until you become my wife." His thumb smoothed the moisture from the kiss-swollen contours of her lips. "The torture will not only be mine."

Her lips trembled as his implacable expression hardened.

"And you won't be leaving my castle—not now, not in the foreseeable future. Is that understood?"

She frowned. "You'll keep me prisoner."

"You'll be free to do the things you've always done in my employ."

"Except leave," she said between clenched teeth.

"Aye, that's the way of it." With that, he turned and walked over the Sterrm, waiting for her so he could boost her into the saddle.

After a moment of almost shaking with anger, Frances let herself be boosted into the saddle. And in the time it took to return to the castle, had already come up with several different ways to leave.

CHAPTER EIGHT

*D*espite the cold, Frances muffled herself in a thick jacket and scarf, ready for her walk, unsurprised to see Fergus at the edge of the outer wall. She'd had an escort any time she left the inside of the castle.

"Miss Rothbury."

Frances nodded. "Fergus."

"The Laird requests you not walk this morning on account of the Gathering today. He wishes to see you in private before it starts."

She let out a careful breath but nodded again and gathered her scarf closer to her chin as she made her way back along the outer wall of the castle. It was freezing, but she still walked as much as she could. In the two weeks after their time at the cottage, life had gone on as normal.

Except her every move was watched.

The Laird was good as his word. She wasn't going to get any chance to escape. Lord knows she'd tried every sneaky way she could think of but had been thwarted at every turn.

Their time at the cabin had been short but steeped in so much sensuality she couldn't help the blush on her cheeks the whole way back.

But the worst thing had been the Laird asking for her hand in marriage.

Even now, the memory of it made her stop and lean against the stone wall, her eyes seeing nothing of the forest covered in white in front of her. She closed her eyes, the biting cold stinging her cheeks. The need to leave warred with her want for a man and his family she could never have.

The ride back to the castle had been silent, and he'd since treated her with a calm courtesy made worse given the heated memories branded in her consciousness. There was nothing in his demeanour to suggest anything explicit had happened. But Frances knew.

In the dark of night, the heat pooling in her blood and beneath her skin knew.

Opening her eyes, Frances looked at the bits of green poking through the snow and the path that beckoned into the forest.

She was weary of being a prisoner.

A prisoner to the beast within.

A prisoner to men who thought they knew best. She turned her back on the weak sunshine and walked into the castle, ready for finality of what lay ahead. For when the Gathering finished, she would be asking Malcolm to help her leave.

"Good morning, Laird Grant."

"Miss Rothbury."

Her lips tightened at the hint of darkness in his tone. And the silence that followed.

"You wished to see me?" she prompted, her voice calm.

Duncan leaned back in the carved, wooden chair, watching her with a speculative gaze. "Have you thought any more of my proposal, Miss Rothbury?

She'd thought of nothing else. Heavier than lead, her heart sank but in a clear voice, she said the words she knew she should. "I have. And my answer is the same. It's for the best that I do not accept your offer."

The silence ensued again.

A log burning in the fireplace shifted and the fire popped in a shower of sparks.

"The best for whom?"

Frances swallowed as she struggled to retain her calm. "You do me a great honour, Laird Grant. But I cannot accept—"

He made a disgusted sound. "I love you as you are, here and *now*."

The vow, spoken in his deep voice cracked open her façade as every muscle in her body went rigid. Clenching her teeth together, she swallowed, desperately trying to claw back her composure.

"My children love you, as you love them. How can you leave them?"

Oh, that was not fair. Tears pooled in her eyes. "I...I cannot marry you," she said, her voice hoarse as she forced the words out.

His gaze narrowed. "I see."

Her skin prickled as the tension in the room increased.

"I have information that satisfies some of the questions I've had about your story."

It was hard to breathe in a normal fashion. Frances felt as though fists were squeezing her lungs. "What information?"

"I contacted my solicitor to enquire about you some time ago. He sent his man to London to investigate."

Frances couldn't speak, her heart in her throat. He'd had her investigated?

"He returned last week and my solicitor has sent me his report." Duncan sat forward, his gaze pinning her to the spot as she stood before him. "Lord Ashburn has a well-known reputation. Four maids of his employ have been wronged; one is pregnant, two have children, his bastards. One maid has been found dead, although no one has come forth to accuse him of course."

Her lips trembling, Frances clenched her teeth together to stop them from chattering. Those poor women. They'd had the same experience as she'd had but lacked the strength to stop him from rape. For a moment, she was intensely glad she'd killed him. No more women would suffer a horrible fate—

"But it seems the Lord has had to permanently retire to his country estate after suffering an undisclosed injury. And it is rumoured he has gone mad. His wife is too ashamed to be seen in London."

For a moment, Frances didn't comprehend, and then gasped as the realisation hit her. "I…I didn't kill him?"

"Nay. You didn't kill him, sweetling. And there are no Lord's men or redcoats looking for you."

"God in heaven," she whispered, unable to believe it.

"I've also discovered that your real name is Lydia Spencer, *Lady Spencer*."

Shock made her blink as she stopped breathing. *Her name. Her real name, spoken for the first time in so long...*

"And since the death of your brother, that you're the sole benefactor of your parent's estate after they perished some time ago in a carriage accident. They were the Viscount and Lady Spencer?"

As her poor heart suffered another jolt, Frances' nodded in a daze.

"You and your brother were duped into believing a distant cousin had inherited the estate by your parent's solicitor. The fraud was discovered almost two years after the death of your parents, but by then, you'd disappeared."

"How did…?"

Nodding, Duncan agreed. "Aye, the investigator was thorough."

Frances shook her head in disbelief, trying to understand.

"There's one more thing, Lady Spencer."

Her stunned gaze found his.

"Your grandmother is still alive, and is travelling en route to Muckrach Castle, although the journey will be slow due to her age."

Frances tried but failed to stifle a small cry. "My g-grandmother? She's coming to here?"

"She's in fine health and eager to meet the granddaughter she's never met, to instruct her on the heritage denied to her since she was born. So you see, there's reason to stay after all."

Her Grandmother! She had a family.

Tears pooled in Frances' eyes and she pressed trembling fingers to her mouth. Her childhood memories of any mention of her grandmother had not been kind. "She really wants to see me?"

"Aye, she's written you a letter."

"Laird Grant. I-I don't know what to say. How can I—"

A knock at the door halted her stumbling words and she swung around as the door opened.

"Laird Grant, 'tis time to begin the Gathering." Malcolm's indifferent voice cut across her wobbling gratitude like a sword thrust.

Heat climbed into her cheeks and she stammered, "Of course, I'm so sorry. Taking too much of your time. The Gathering. I…I can't thank you enough, Laird. Long will you have my…my gratitude."

Frances dropped a small curtsey and began backing away.

Giving Malcolm a glare, Duncan said, "Miss Spencer, *Lady* Spencer, I'll be making arrangements once the Gathering is done."

Dismissed, she left the room in a hurry, her mind whirling with the information she'd just received. Duncan had done this for her. Duncan had sent his man to investigate. *Duncan…*

Frances stopped and leaned against the wall, her thoughts in a jumble, trying to take it all in.

All this time, she'd never been in any real danger, no Lord's men after her. She had let fear rule every moment since she'd fled the Lord's estate. Inhaling a skipping breath, she remembered his words.

"…I love you as you are, here and now…"

Closing her eyes, tried to understand what Duncan meant. But then, footsteps echoed in the hallway. Lifting her skirts, she hurried on to the main hall, where the children would be waiting for her.

There were lots of people crammed into the main hall, adding more warmth to the chill of the day. The Laird strode through the crowd, greeting people by name, shaking hands and clapping their backs.

Lowering her lashes, Frances hid the longing she could feel with each breath she inhaled. In full clan colours, he was the only man for her. She could barely look at him lest everyone know the clamour that rang in her blood.

Brodie's hand tightened around hers and she looked down at him. Despite his expressionless face, he was nervous. She could tell, and her heart broke a little when he looked up at her.

Nodding, she smiled. "Master Brodie, you must take your place with your father now. The crowd is beginning to settle."

For a moment, he didn't move. She smiled again, a soft encouraging smile. "Go on, now, lad. You'll do."

She saw him square his shoulders and then his

hand slipped from hers. The loss had her drawing in a painful breath, and she was assailed by the sudden aching reality of what it was going to feel when she left. For a moment she couldn't breathe. *Like ripping her heart out to leave it beating on the ground.*

The Laird stood when Brodie settled beside him, and then walked forward and began speaking in Gaelic. The sound of his deep voice immediately halted all chatter as the crowd listened.

"He's welcoming everyone, and naming the clans," whispered Mrs Cullen.

Frances glanced down at the smaller woman with a grateful smile. And so it went on. Mrs Cullen translated as grievances were aired. Malcolm called out names and one by one, people of the clan came forward. Duncan was fair, sometimes hard, but always fair. And she was proud of Brodie, who never fidgeted, but took his place to learn from his father.

"Frances Rothbury."

Startled, she looked up at Malcolm's cold tone to where he stood as his Laird's second. Frances didn't move, her heart in her throat. Her mind had gone blank as she stood frozen.

The silence was oppressive.

"Go on, lass." Mrs Cullen looked worried as she gave Frances a small push. Frances walked on wooden legs to the centre of the space in front of the Laird.

Duncan spoke in Gaelic, and Malcolm translated. "Miss Rothbury. Turn to face the people."

For the first time, she looked at Duncan. His expression told her nothing, but determination rolled off him in waves.

What was he going to do?

"Turn, Miss Rothbury."

Frances swallowed hard, and slowly turned. Holding her head high, she met the gazes of the

Laird's people, hoping her own expression didn't give away her fear.

Duncan addressed the crowd and Malcolm said, "The Laird would like it known first, to those of his clan and to those who give allegiance to the Clan Grant, of his intention to marry this woman."

Oh, *God!*

A wave of almost painful heat swept into her cheeks. She refused to look down, but hidden in her skirts, her hand clenched so tightly, she felt her nails dig painfully into her skin.

He wanted to marry her still?

Duncan spoke again, the liquid syllables of the language she did not know addressed to her back.

Malcolm's tone was cold and emotionless. "The Laird advises that Miss Frances Rothbury is actually Lady Lydia Frances Spencer and should thus be addressed."

Amidst the sudden murmuring, Frances struggled with her vulnerability. Every muscle in her body went rigid as black spots danced in front of her eyes. But then she took an uneven breath, as much as she could and the black spots disappeared.

She turned her head to look back at him.

His stern expression softened as the barest smile stretched his lips.

He had done so much for her, and despite everything, loved her as she was. *I love you as you are, here and now.* In that moment, she understood and the love she felt for him threatened to explode; she could feel her blood fizzing with the emotion.

And he saw. His smile deepened, his eyes flared and he nodded. "Turn and face the clan, Lady Spencer."

She turned and saw Mrs Cullen wiping her eyes.

The Laird spoke and then there was a pause.

Slowly, people started to raise their hand and Frances frowned when no translation followed.

The he spoke in English. "The Laird asks the people of clan Grant: who raises their hand in favour of the marriage between Lydia Spencer and himself?"

Everyone had raised their hand.

Duncan spoke again. "The Laird asks the people of clan Grant to so say *aye*, to the marriage between Lady Spencer and himself."

A resounding *aye* echoed through the hall.

And then a single resounding *nay*.

Her heart skipped a beat. Frances turned.

"Malcolm." The Laird said his name, his voice cool, the warning clear. "State the reason for your nay."

Malcolm started to speak in Gaelic.

Duncan stopped him. "English. So we *all* can understand your rejection."

Malcolm slowly walked towards Frances. "She is English."

"So was my last wife."

"Aye, Laird, not strong enough to survive here. She doesn't belong here, especially given her recently elevated status."

A murmur swept the crowd, and Frances saw a few whispering with others.

Malcolm continued, "All remember when Marie died in childbirth with your daughter Roslyn. But she was sickly from the time she arrived."

"Lady Spencer hasn't so much as sneezed since she's been here, despite walking the woods in the dead of winter. What is amiss, Malcolm?"

There were a few titters and then silence.

Malcolm had reached her, standing behind her.

"She's English, and *titled*. Why was she hiding it? What other secrets does she carry?"

Frances looked back and Duncan's gaze on her

hardened. "Lady Spencer was attacked by an English Lord while as a governess in his employ."

There were shocked gasps from some.

"Aye. She travelled here under a different identity to escape his clutches." Duncan looked around the room at each of his clan. "And she's given herself to this clan in a myriad of selfless ways."

There was strong *ayes* and nods, backing up Duncan's implacable statement. And then he smiled. "Anyone who sees her with my children does not doubt."

All nodded and there was a resounding *aye*.

Even before it happened, Frances knew it was going to; Malcolm was losing the clan's approval. The level of emotion coming from him was so thick, it almost choked her.

Suddenly, his strong arm came around her neck, squeezing to impede her breath.

"Malcolm! No!" Duncan lunged towards them, drawing his sword, and was followed by at least a dozen of his men. Shocked gasps filled the air.

Frances lifted her hands to Malcolm's muscular arm but when a sharp prick stung her ribs, she subsided.

Malcolm wrenched her to the side, his back to the wall as he dragged her to protect his flank.

Duncan froze when Malcolm lifted the knife and Frances stiffened and inhaled sharply as the point went deeper into her skin. More men moved forward with careful steps, their swords out.

"Malcolm, stop! This is not you! You protect all the women." Duncan bellowed.

An angry murmur swept through the crowd.

"Let us see the real Lady Spencer!" Malcolm growled it next to her ear.

Duncan tore his gaze from his most trusted and loyal friend to her, and Frances could see the anguish in his eyes. He was helpless and she knew why. Malcolm wasn't going to kill her, he was going to force her to reveal the *beserker*. Already, she could feel the ice encasing her heart, its tendrils freezing her veins, readying itself to protect.

But when she looked into Duncan's eyes, she could see his love, the determination to protect her—a lifetime of love, for her, as she was.

"Don't you hurt Miss Rothbury!"

Her gaze went to Brodie, who had a sword he could barely lift in his hands. An upsurge of love so strong and pure spilled out of her heart and cold ebbed.

"Aye, don't you hurt my gov'ness. You're a *bad* man, Malcolm." Roslyn echoed her brother.

She was loved. *Loved!* A kind of stillness came over her and she inhaled deeply as a sense of peace saturated her entire being. The *beserker* was in her, it *was her*. It was hers to control, not the other way around.

"Malcolm." She said his name quietly as she shielded her lashes.

"Shut up, witch," he growled, in her ear. She felt his pain and his rage and deliberately opened her senses. An image of a woman, with more delicate features than his…his sister, a beloved sister. From a little girl to when she'd bloomed into a woman. And then the horror of finding her dead, torn and bloody.

This time she did not ignore her gift and shy away from it, but welcomed it and learned from it.

Gwenneth. Gwennie. That was her name.

She understood instantly. "Oh, Malcolm," she said softly, "Your sister Gwenneth was so beautiful, an angel. And she loved you so."

He jerked and point of the knife dug into her ribs. Frances flinched but kept her voice soft. "I'm so sorry for your loss, and the senselessness of what happened to her."

"Shut up!" Malcolm roared.

The gathering went silent.

"You know nothing…" his voice broke.

Frances allowed the *beserker* strength to infuse her muscles. For the first time, she controlled it, channelled it to where she wanted. She pulled his arm from her neck and herself from knife, and turned to face him.

She deliberately raised her lashes and looked at him, showing him the icy pain she lived with at all times.

He jerked and swallowed, unable to look away from her iridescent, glowing eyes.

"Malcolm. Carrying so much pain can make you blind. I should know. It took your Laird to show me that letting go of fear and rage and allowing yourself to love is its own reward."

"You don't love him…even he said so, that you'd rejected his offer of marriage. As though you're too good for him. For us!"

She bought her cold hand softly to his face and cradled his cheek.

He flinched, his gaze cleaving to hers, his mouth working as he frowned at the chill phenomenon.

Frances lowered her voice. "Too good for him? No, he is too good for *me*."

His eyes widened at her words.

"Yes, I refused his offer of marriage, because I'm a *monster*. This is what I am. You, the clan—you're people of such love and kindness. You took me in and made me feel part of your family."

She let the anguish out in an agonised whisper, "How could I say yes and endanger you all? After the Gathering, I was going to seek you out…so…so you could help me leave."

Frances stifled a sob, thencollected herself.

Malcolm searched her gaze, seeking an answer she didn't know if she had, something to satisfy whatever demon drove him. She could only wait.

"Frances." Duncan said.

She shook her head, a silent request for him to wait.

Outside, the wind had risen, the snow coming down in gusty flurries as it howled around castle, a physical counterpoint to the tension sweeping the room.

His harsh voice vibrated with fury. "You harm her Malcolm, and I'll kill you."

The tension in the already tense hall, increased ten-fold.

Frances whispered, "I love Duncan so much, *I would die for him.* I would kill anyone who dares hurt any one of you. I *have killed to protect his children.*"

"You…you love him?"

She took a deep breath and nodded. "With all that I am. If you wish it, Malcolm, I will turn to face the clan—*your people*—and show them the monster I am if you think it best. You're the brother of his heart and he needs you and your loyalty more than he needs me."

Pain twisted Malcolm's expression as he looked into her eyes and then closed his tightly.

"Letting go of your rage does not mean you forget your beautiful sister, nor her memory. You did not fail her, Malcolm. You did not *fail her.*" Frances dug her fingers gently into his skin. "You *must* let go of your guilt and let the light in."

He said nothing.

Frances inhaled, then let out her breath as her heart sank. She stepped back, her hand falling from his face, and went to turn.

But his hand caught the crook of her elbow. "Stop."

She looked up at him.

Malcolm shuddered, his dark features full of anguish. "I am…I have been wrong. Forgive me," he ground out, his voice thick with emotion.

Frances pulled him into her embrace, feeling his arms go around her, and let the ice inside disperse. He was an armful, considering he was the same size and height of Duncan. Suddenly, another vision slid into her mind and she stilled for a moment, her breath coming in shallow gusts.

Then she leaned toward his ear and whispered, "The one who murdered your sister. You will face them in your future."

Malcolm raised his head, his beautiful green eyes glittering with unshed tears. "You-you've seen this? Who?"

Her eyes narrowed and she nodded. "Yes. I cannot see who, but I know you will face them."

"Your word," he demanded, his voice hoarse.

Her gaze softened. "On my word, Malcolm, for what it's worth."

Nodding once, he inhaled deeply and blinked away the betraying moisture. He took her arm and led her back to the Laird.

Then he knelt, taking his knife in both hands, held it outstretched and bowed his head. "Aye to the marriage between the Laird and Frances Spencer. I offer my life for threatening another of the Clan. You both have my fealty, my loyalty and my sword to the Clan Grant, to protect you, its people and any children that come after you."

Frances looked at Duncan, seeing the deep anger at his best friend's actions.

She put her hand on Malcolm's shoulder, and her

other hand on Duncan's arm. Giving him a look, she gradually pushed the arm holding the sword down.

Duncan eventually sheathed his sword. "I accept your fealty, your loyalty and your sword for the Clan, Malcolm. There will be no bloodshed on this day. Rise."

As one, the clan clapped and cheered. Duncan shook his friend's hand, then drew him forward to clap him on the back and said in a soft voice, "I'm going to thrash you to within an inch of your life for harming my soon to be wife."

Looking as though he'd been to hell, Malcolm nodded. "It's no less than I deserve."

Duncan nodded, his expression severe. "Call for the vote again."

Once more, he nudged Frances forward and Malcolm took his place beside the Laird.

Frances turned to face the crowd, almost dizzy with emotion as she looked at the clan. *Her* clan, if she had the courage.

Could she?

"The Laird again asks the people of clan Grant to so say *aye*, to the marriage to Frances Spencer."

This time the *aye* was so loud it shook the rafters. There was a deafening silence that followed.

Tears blurred her vision as she pressed her fingers to her trembling lips.

Warm hands turned her, and she looked up at the Duncan's beloved face as she blinked through her tears.

In a quiet voice, only for her, he asked, "The Laird asks Lady Frances Spencer, does she so say *aye* to a marriage with Laird Grant?"

The temptation was strong, but the word trembled on her lips as the fear she'd lived with all of her life still rose. *What if she—?*

"The Laird promises to protect and love Frances

Spencer, but only if she in turn, swears to protect the Laird, his children and his people."

Her breath caught as she saw the look in his eyes, that determination, the love, the heat of his desire.

"The Laird will not accept the marriage if Frances Spencer cannot protect him, his children and his people."

Her heart was so full. She knew what he was saying—he wanted her, *beserker* and all. The last of the frozen wall of fear around her heart melted under a fierce blast of love and gave her the courage and hope for the future.

Wetting her dry lips, she cleared her throat and said, "Aye."

He grinned, his grey eyes lightening to almost diamond brilliance. "The Laird asks you say it louder, for the people to hear."

Frances felt her lips stretch in a smile as delight fizzed in her blood. She took a deep breath and said in a loud, strong voice, "Aye!"

The clan erupted in thunderous cheers and Duncan caught her in an embrace that threatened to crack her ribs. She didn't care, her arms coming up around his neck to hold him just as fiercely.

"I love you. I'm never letting you go," she said in his ear.

"You're mine *sassenach*. Mine to protect and keep safe, by God." He said it against her ear, and she shivered as his warm breath feathered against the sensitive lobe.

"And you're mine to protect and keep safe, too. All of you," she whispered against his.

He kissed her, and the noise faded; all she felt were his strong arms and his mouth on hers.

Until two little arms wrapped around her hips. She eased away from Duncan and looked down to see Roslyn hugging her tight.

Duncan lifted his daughter and Frances looked for Brodie, finding him on the other side of her.

"You're not leaving us?" Almost identical to his father, his impassive face tugged at her heart.

With her other arm, she dragged him to her for a hug, dropping a smacking kiss on his forehead. "No, Brodie. You're my family and I am *never* leaving you. Ever."

The clan surrounded them, full of good cheer. And Frances smiled until her cheeks ached. She looked up at Duncan. For a heartbeat, she allowed her eyes to glow, a flash of iridescent blue before demurely lowering her lashes.

He spoke softly into her ear, "Meet me in the library, later. There's a book I'd like to show you."

She grinned and he cupped her face. "I love you."

Rising on tippie toes, she kissed him, her arms full of children and him. Her heart, empty and cold for so long, now overflowed with warmth and love.

EPILOGUE

A few weeks later...

Dinner conversation in the hall was in full swing but Lydia still heard Roslyn over the din.

'Mama! Brodie stole my apple pie!'

Lydia looked over at Brodie and bit her lip to stop an incipient grin. His attempt at looking innocent was always comical.

'I didn't,' he protested, but it was a half-hearted attempt. He sighed, then gave his plate to Roslyn, who promptly poked her tongue at him.

Lydia looked at Brodie closely, noting the leanness of his cheeks and a sudden realisation came to her.

'Brodie—' Duncan started, but she laid a hand on his arm and rose.

'Trust me,' she whispered in his ear as she passed.

She bade Brodie to follow her to a quieter corner of the hall, where she they couldn't be overheard by all who were enjoying the evening.

'Young man, are you still hungry?'

He dropped his gaze and nodded. 'Yes.'

Lydia curved gentle fingers around his chin so his

gaze once more came to hers. 'You are growing so fast. It's no wonder. Come, we'll ask for more food.'

Brodie nodded his hand creeping up to clutch hers as they walked to the kitchen. Lydia swallowed but didn't say anything, despite feeling as though his hand was clutching her heart. He was a quiet, stoic boy, but she could see he was about to jump into adolescence. No wonder he was hungry.

'You mustn't steal your sister's dessert, Brodie,' she chided gently, but her heart wasn't in the rebuke.

'Yes. I'm sorry.'

She looked down at him with a smile. 'Mrs Cullen does makes a fine apple pie, doesn't she?'

Brodie grinned.

Lydia pushed open the heavy oak door that keep the heat and ruckus of the kitchen from reaching the banquet hall. 'If you're hungry, come and tell me. I'll make sure you have enough.'

When he nodded, looking up at her with such adoration, her fingers tightened around his. Her heart, already full, swelled even more. Had she ever thought she could be so…fulfilled? This life here, with Duncan and his children was everything she'd never dared to imagine.

A few minutes and a heaped plate later, they returned to the revelries and she took her place once more with Duncan.

'Is Brodie well?'

Lydia nodded as she sat. 'Yes. Though he's going to need more food, much more. Your boy is growing so fast now.'

Duncan looked at his son tucking into his food, then back at her. 'You can always see to the heart of the matter, where others would scold. I love you more every day.' He leaned over and pulled her into his arms, kissing her full on the lips.

'Yer not married yet, Laird!' Donal called out.

Everyone laughed, and Lydia pulled back, her cheeks warm. Duncan grinned, warmth radiating from his handsome features as he bent to whisper in her ear, 'You're blushing but you're eyes are sparkling like jewels. It won't be long until we're married. Your Grandmother and cousin should be arriving any day now.'

Her gaze searched his. The noise of the hall faded and she let out sigh as her fingers sought his big, strong hand. 'I came here a frightened woman, with no prospects. Some days I feel it's like a dream and I pinch myself for reassurance. I can't tell you how happy you've made me.'

The smile slowly left his face as his gaze grew intense. Raising her hand, he kissed her fingers, and said in a low voice full of emotion. 'Nay, my Lady. Tis you who have brought happiness to everyone, but most especially to me. I love you.'

'I love you more,' she whispered as their foreheads met.

'Laird! Get a room!' Fergus yelled.

The laughter of the clan filled the entire hall, hers included, and Duncan turned as Donal slapped his back.

Any reservations about the clan's acceptance of her were gone, replaced with a pride in the lady who'd defended and protected the Laird's children with her own life. The sense of belonging she felt with these people—her people—was overwhelming. All of them were her family, where she'd had none for so long.

Until she saw *him*, walking the edge of the shadows in the hall. The darkness seemed to hug his form as moved swiftly in the gloom.

Malcolm.

In these last few weeks, she'd only seen him once. And that was after Duncan had soundly thrashed him for daring to harm her. She'd been horrified but Malcolm had been adamant that the Laird had no choice. T'was the way they settled wrong-doings and disputes and no less than he deserved, he'd said.

Uneasiness rose, as it always did when he appeared. Something surrounded Malcolm, other than the vengeance he sought for those who murdered his sister. Something dark, something she couldn't quite see…

Protect. Family.

The words rang like a clarion in her head.

Lydia sucked in a shaky breath and rose, compelled to walk swiftly to where Malcolm was skirting the wall, clearly intending to leave.

This time he would not escape.

She caught him just inside the edge of the hallway which led to the back of the castle. 'Malcolm.'

He stopped then turned to face her with a look not unlike Brodie, when she'd caught him doing something he shouldn't. Mayhap it would take longer for him to reconcile his feelings for her as the Lady of the castle.

'You are leaving so soon?'

'Aye, my Lady.'

She was heartened by his normal tone; unlike before there was no animosity in his voice, no quips or barbs. 'Lydia,' she invited.

He remained silent.

'How are your ribs?' she pressed.

His expression remained impassive. 'They are fine, my…Lady.'

'Lydia, Malcolm.' She dug her heels in. 'I hear you are visiting the widow Aird tomorrow?'

His expression grew wary. 'Aye.'

She smiled. He would not hold her at a distance. He was like a brother to Duncan, an integral part of the Clan, and the sooner he learned his position had not changed, the better. The sooner he learned all of Duncan's clan would be cared for, the better, too.

'I have a basket for you to take for her and Kenzie. Is that the young woman's name who lives with the widow? Will you take it with you?'

He nodded, some of the wariness leaching from his expression. And then the barest smile. 'Aye, her name is Kenzie. I'll deliver your basket.'

She beamed at him. It was a small step, but considering how they'd begun, it felt like a big leap forward.

'Thank you, Malcolm. Maybe next time you visit I can come with—' the words halted as she gasped at a sudden dizziness which struck with vicious strength. Reaching out blindly, she grabbed his arm as she swayed.

'My Lady? Lydia?' he asked, his tone urgent as he held her steady.

Malcolm. Protect. My. Family.

'It's you,' she whispered. And when the dizziness abated, she looked at him with wide eyes. 'Malcolm, you must promise me.'

'Promise you?'

Lydia tried to understand what the warning meant, even as it waned and disappeared into the ether. But an urgent foreboding clutched at her throat, and she gripped his arm tighter, barely able to speak. 'Duncan says my grandmother should be arriving within the day.' She looked up at him. 'I sense danger. You must protect my family, Malcolm. Only you can.'

His eyes searched hers. And whatever he saw there had him nodding. 'Aye, my Lady. I'll protect them. You have my word.'

'Thank you.' Lydia closed her eyes, the words fervent and shaky.

'Lydia?' She opened her eyes to see Duncan

striding towards them, taking her from Malcolm as soon as he was in reach, and holding her close. 'What is amiss?'

His questioning gaze was fixed on Malcolm, clearly wanting an answer.

'I think she's had another vision,' Malcolm answered.

Duncan looked down at her with a frown. 'Are you well?'

She nodded, able to breathe again after the dreadful sensation passed. 'Yes, I'm better. I had a vision of sorts, but not a very clear one.'

Duncan grasped Malcolm's arm briefly. 'My thanks, Malcolm.'

Malcolm nodded, 'My Lady, Laird.' After giving a swift half bow, he strode down the long, shadowed hall.

'We cannot go back just yet, love. Your eyes are still glowing.' Duncan said softly, his hand softly tracing her back.

Laying her head on his chest, Lydia watched Malcolm disappear into the darkness and murmured, 'Danger surrounds him, Duncan.' She then looked up at him. 'And it now surrounds us all.'

I do hope you enjoyed reading **The Governess**. Stay tuned for more about the Beserkers of Muckrach Castle with Malcolm's story, **The Protector**, coming soon!

Keep reading for a sneak peek of the **The Sentinel.**

THE SENTINEL

'I have you ...so you're mine to hold...'

Captain of the Sentinel Guard, Ciaran rarely uses his magic for fear of awakening his dark, primal side. But when his King is kidnapped and tortured, Ciaran's power alone will not be enough, and he must invoke his magic to compel a powerful empath healer —one who denies her magic exists. One who defies him with every breath she takes. One who denies the passion between them.

Submit to a man? Never again...

After believing she had killed her violent husband, Empath Healer Charys has no time for men, nor her magic. The worst thing one of her kind can do is to kill another. Believing herself unworthy of her gift, she shuns all who request her help. Even the Captain of the Sentinel Guard, whom she knows has a power much greater than her own. But she doesn't count on the power of her own desires.

By joining their magic, the battle to save the King begins. So too, does the battle of wills.

Who will be the first to give in?